The Haunting of Tram Car 015

ALSO BY P. DJÈLÍ CLARK

The Black God's Drums

THE HAUNTING OF TRAM CAR 015

P. DJÈLÍ CLARK

A TOM DOHERTY ASSOCIATES BOOK

NEW YORK

THE HAUNTING OF TRAM CAR 015

Copyright © 2019 by P. Djèlí Clark
Excerpt copyright © 2018 by P. Djèlí Clark

Cover art by Stephan Martiniere
Cover design by Christine Foltzer

Edited by Diana M. Pho

A Tor.com Book
Published by Tom Doherty Associates
175 Fifth Avenue
New York, NY 10010

www.tor.com

Tor® is a registered trademark of
Macmillan Publishing Group, LLC.

ISBN 978-1-250-29478-4 (ebook)
ISBN 978-1-250-29480-7 (trade paperback)

First Edition: February 2019

For Nia & Nya, who took on an al and won.
Our little fighters.

The Haunting of Tram Car 015

CHAPTER ONE

The office of the Superintendent of Tram Safety & Maintenance at Ramses Station had all the decor befitting someone who had been elevated—or likely pushed along the lines of patronage—into such a vaulted position. A sprawling vintage Anatolian rug of blue angular motifs, red spandrels, and golden tulips bordered in deep lavender. A hanging painting by one of the new abstract pharaonists, with its irregular shapes, splotches, and vivid colors that no one could truly understand. A framed photograph of the king, naturally. And some conveniently placed novels by the most recent Alexandrian writers, their leather-bound covers looking as unopened as the day they'd been bought.

Unfortunately, Agent Hamed Nasr noted with the meticulous eye of an investigator, the superintendent's contrived attempts at good taste were subsumed under the humdrum tediousness of a mid-level bureaucratic functionary: transit maps and line timetables, mechanical schematics and repair schedules, memorandums and reports, all overlaid one upon another on washed-out yellow walls like decaying dragon scales. They flapped carelessly beneath the air of an oscillating copper fan, its spinning blades rattling inside its cage as if trying to get out. And somehow, still, it was stifling in here, so that Hamed had to resist the urge to pull at the neckband of his white collarless shirt—thankful, at least, that the dark uniform he wore concealed any signs of perspiration in the lingering heat of late-summer Cairo.

The office's proprietor was seated in a high-backed chair behind a stained, coffee-colored desk. It showed signs of wear, and a fine crack led up one leg where the wood had been split. But its owner had taken care to keep it polished, so that it gleamed under the lone flickering gas lamp in the windowless room. He didn't seem bothered by the unbearable climate. Much like his noisy fan, he prattled on, impervious.

"It's odd that we call it a tram system," he intoned. His finger stood poised beneath a bold nose sheltering a waxed moustache streaked with gray that twisted and curved up at the ends. Hamed was amazed by the man's pomposity: behaving as if he were lecturing first-year students at university—and not speaking to agents of the Ministry of Alchemy, Enchantments, and Supernatural Entities. "It is really a telpher system, when you think on it clearly," he droned on. "Trams are pulled along a single cable line. But like telphers, our cars move independently along any given line, even switching lines at given points much like a train. The original telpher was invented in London back in the 1880s. But once our djinn got ahold of the idea, the mechanics were greatly expanded upon."

"Absolutely fascinating, Superintendent Bashir!" a younger man seated beside Hamed exclaimed. At twenty-four, only four years younger in truth. But the round, clean brown face beneath his Ministry-issued red tarboosh looked as if it belonged on a boy. At the moment, he was rapt with both attention and genuine interest.

"Oh indeed!" The superintendent's head bobbed like some windup toy, eager for the audience. "People have little understanding of how the transit system that connects much of Cairo works. Not to mention what has to be planned for the future. A city of over two million and growing is going to require major works to keep up with its population." He reached for a bronze dish on his desk and jerkily offered it forward. "More sudjukh, Agent Onsi?"

The younger man gave his thanks, gleefully grabbing a few more bits of the sweet—a brown concoction of hardened syrup and nuts that tasted of cloves and cinnamon. The superintendent presented the dish to Hamed, who politely declined. He'd been fighting to get one of the things unstuck from his teeth for the past few minutes.

"Delicious!" Onsi said, crunching down on a mouthful. "Where did you say these were from, Superintendent?"

"Armenia!" The man beamed, drawing out the word. "I visited last year on a development trip with the Transportation Bureau. The government hopes increased modernizations will assure stability for the republic, after so much hardship brokering their independence. While there, I absolutely fell in love with the local food. Sudjukh is by far my favorite."

"Sudjukh," Onsi mouthed as he chewed, his bushy eyebrows furrowing above a pair of round wire-rimmed silver spectacles. "I always thought that was a type of cured sausage."

"Ah!" the superintendent exclaimed, leaning his angular body forward. "You may be thinking of sujuk! The spelling is sometimes similar, though the pronunciation—"

Hamed cleared his throat loudly, coughing into his short moustache. If he had to sit through a conversation about the dried meats of Transcaucasia, he just might go insane. Or be forced to eat his foot. One or the other. And he liked both his sanity and his feet. Catching the superintendent's attention, he spared a remonstrative glance for Onsi. They were here on Ministry business, not to spend the morning chatting idly like old men at a coffee shop.

"Superintendent Bashir," he began, trying to smooth

the impatience in his voice into something more diplomatic—and scoot a bit of sudjukh from between his molars. "If you could tell us about the problem you're having with the tram?"

The man blinked, as if just remembering why they were there.

"Yes, yes, of course," he answered, sitting back into his chair with a huff. He fiddled with the blue-striped kaftan that he wore over a crisp white gallabiyah, the latter complete with buttons and a shirt collar, after the ministerial fashion. Pulling a kerchief from a front pocket, he mopped at the perspiration on his forehead. "It is all such dreadful business," he complained. "Well, there's no way to put this politely—the tram is haunted!"

Hamed opened his notepad, sighing under his breath as he jotted down the word "haunting." That's what had been typed on the file that landed on his desk this morning. He'd hoped the case might turn out to be something more interesting. But a haunting it was going to be. He stopped writing, looking up as his mind worked out what the man had just said.

"Wait, your *tram* is haunted?"

The superintendent answered with a dour nod that made his moustache droop. "Tram 015, that runs the line down to the Old City. It's one of the newer models that came out in 1910. Only two years in service, and we're already having these troubles. God protect us!"

"I didn't know trams could be haunted," Onsi murmured, plopping another sudjukh in his mouth.

Hamed had to agree. He'd heard of haunted buildings. Haunted homes. Even had a case once of a haunted mausoleum in al-Qarafa, which was rather silly when you thought about it. Why make your home a cemetery, then complain about hauntings? But a haunted tram car? That was new.

"Oh, it's quite haunted," the superintendent assured. "Passengers have encountered the spirit on several occasions. We'd hoped perhaps it would just leave on its own accord. But now it's attacked a woman, just yesterday! She was able to escape unharmed, praise be to God. But not before her clothing was all but ripped to shreds!"

Onsi sat gawking until Hamed cleared his throat again. The younger man jumped at that, fumbling out his own notepad to begin scribbling.

"How long has this been going on?" Hamed asked.

The superintendent looked down to a calendar on his desk, tapping the days contemplatively. "This was the first report just over a week ago, from a mechanic. The man has an ill moral character: a drinker and a carouser. His work chief believed he'd arrived at his station drunk. Almost wrote him up for dismissal, until the passenger complaints began arriving." He motioned to a small stack of papers nearby. "Soon we were hearing from other mechanics. Why, I've seen the wicked thing myself!"

"What did you do?" Onsi asked, drawn in by the tale.

"What any right-standing man would," the superintendent replied, puffing up. "I informed the foul spirit I was a Muslim, and there is but One God, and so it could do me no harm! After that, a few other men took my lead, reciting surahs in the hopes of driving it away. Alas, the vexed thing is still here. After the attack, I deemed it best that I call in those who are more skilled in these matters." He patted his chest in a grateful gesture.

Hamed suppressed the urge to roll his eyes. Half of Cairo flooded the Ministry with trivial concerns, jumping at their own shadows. The other half assumed they could handle everything themselves—with a few verses, some amulets and charms, or a bit of folk magic passed down from their teita. "You say you've seen the entity in question," he prodded. "Could you describe it?"

Superintendent Bashir squirmed. "Not precisely. I mean, well, it's difficult to explain. Perhaps I should just show you?"

Hamed nodded, standing and pulling at the hem of his coat. The superintendent followed suit, leading Hamed and Onsi from the small hot room. They walked down a hallway that housed the station's administrative offices before being herded through the gilded silver doors of a lift, where a boilerplate eunuch stood waiting patiently.

"The aerial yard," Bashir instructed.

The machine man's featureless brass face registered no sign of hearing the order, but it sprang into motion—reaching out a mechanical hand to pull on a lever embedded onto the floor. There was the low grumbling of turning gears, like an old man roused from bed, and the lift began to rise. They traveled a short while before the doors opened again, and when Hamed stepped out he had to shield his eyes from the late morning sun.

They were atop Ramses Station where you could see Cairo spread out below: a sprawl of busy streets, spired masjid, factories and architecture that spanned the ages amid the scaffolding of newly rising constructions. The superintendent had the truth of it. The city was growing by the day, from the cramped downtown to the south, to the mansions and well-tended gardens in wealthy Gezira. And that was just on the ground. Because up here was another world entirely.

The pointed steel turrets atop Ramses Station that mimicked golden minarets served as mooring masts for airships. Most of these ships were lightweight dirigibles that shuttled between Cairo and the main port of Alexandria by the hour, discharging passengers from across the Mediterranean and beyond. Some medium-sized crafts sat among them, heading south to Luxor and Aswan and as far as Khartoum. One giant vessel dwarfed the others, hovering impossibly like a small blue oval moon: a six-propeller heavy class that could make uninterrupted trips east to Bengal, down to Capetown, or even across the Atlantic. Most of Cairo, however, got around by less extravagant means.

Corded cable lines stretched across the skyline in every direction, metal vines that curved and bent as they went, interwoven and overlapping the breadth of the city. Aerial trams zipped along their length—leaving bright electric bolts crackling in their wake. The tram system was Cairo's lifeblood, running on a network of arteries and transporting thousands across the bustling metropolis. It was easy to take it for granted when you walked the streets below, not bothering to look up at the rumbling of their passing. But from this vantage, it was hard not to see transit vehicles as a stark symbol of Cairo's celebrated modernity.

"This way, if you please." The superintendent beckoned.

He took the two agents across a narrow walkway like a bridge, away from the airships and the main cable lines, and up several flights of stairs. When they finally stopped they were in a land of trams. Some twenty or more of the cars sat about in neat rows, hanging from cables by their pulleys but otherwise inactive. From somewhere beneath came the sound of other trams in motion, and between the gaps of the platform Hamed could catch glimpses as they streaked by.

"This is one of the main aerial yards," Bashir explained as they went. "Where we put trams to rotate out of service, those needing rest or repair. When 015 started giving trouble, we placed it here."

Hamed looked to where the man was leading. Tram 015 appeared like all the others he'd ever seen: a narrow, rectangular brass box with sectioned glass windows that wrapped nearly all around. It had green and red trim, and two bulbous lanterns on either end encased in cages of densely decorated interlacing stars. The number 015 was embossed in gold lettering that covered a door near the front. As they approached, the superintendent hung back.

"I'll leave matters in your capable hands from here," the man offered.

Hamed thought impishly of insisting he come along and show them how he had bravely stood up to the spirit. But decided against it. No need to be petty. He waved to Onsi and they walked to the car. The door came open at a pull to reveal a small set of steps. There was a gap between the hanging tram and the platform, showing the Cairo streets a far drop below. Trying to ignore the dizzying sight, Hamed placed a booted foot onto the tram and climbed aboard.

He had to duck his tall frame, holding onto his tarboosh, and draw in a set of broad shoulders to clear the narrow doorway. The car rocked slightly at his entrance and jostled again as Onsi came following behind—shorter by at least half a foot but stout enough to be near equal in weight. It wasn't precisely dark inside the tram, but dim. The lamps on the ceiling were on, and the flickering alchemical filaments cast a glare off the silver buttons running down the front of the two men's coats. The crimson velvet curtains at the windows were drawn back, allowing in some sunlight. But there was still a shadowy cast, making the burgundy cushioned seats of the bolted chairs running along either wall seem as black as their uniforms. The air was different too, thicker and cooler than the dry Cairene heat—filling Hamed's nostrils and sitting heavy on his chest. No doubt about it, something was peculiar with Tram 015.

"What's the procedure, Agent Onsi?" he asked.

If the Ministry was going to saddle him with new recruits, he might as well check to see if they'd been trained properly. The younger man, who had been peering about with interest, brightened at the question. "Sir, we should make sure the area is secure and no civilians are in present danger."

"It's an empty tram car, Agent Onsi," Hamed replied. "And I told you, stop calling me sir. You passed your academy exams so you're an agent just like me. This isn't Oxford."

"Ah yes, sir. Sorry, sir." He shook his head, as if trying to clear it of a lifetime of English schooling, which filtered into his accented Arabic. "I mean, Agent Hamed. Ministry procedure says that, taking into account what we've been told, we should make a spectral examination of the area."

Hamed nodded. Trained right after all. He reached into his coat to pull out the small leather case where he kept his spectral goggles. The copper-plated instruments were standard Ministry issue. They fit like eyeglasses, though the pronounced round green lenses were far wider. Onsi had removed his spectacles to slip on his own pair. Eyesight mattered little when it came to the spectral world—which appeared the same to everyone in a haze of startlingly vivid, luminescent jade. The brocaded flower patterns on the cushioned seats could be seen in detail, along with the golden calligraphy that ran along the black window panes. But what stood out more than anything was the ceiling. Craning to look up, Hamed couldn't fault Onsi for his breathy gasp.

The curved ceiling of the tram was awash in a spectral glow. It came from a complex arrangement of cogwheels covering the entire space. Some of the gears meshed with one another, their teeth interlocking. Others were conjoined by chains into sprockets. They spun and rotated in multiple directions at once, sending out swirling eddies of light. Trams didn't require conductors, not even a boilerplate eunuch. The djinn had created them to run by themselves, to plow along their routes like messenger birds sent on an errand, and this intricate clockwork machinery was their brain.

"I say," Onsi asked, "is that supposed to be there?"

Hamed squinted, following his gaze. There was something moving amid the spinning gearwheels. A bit of ethereal light. He pulled up his goggles and saw it clearly with the naked eye—a sinuous form the color of grayish smoke. It slithered about, like an eel who made its home in a bed of coral. No, that was definitely *not* supposed to be there.

"What's the next step for first encounters with an unknown supernatural entity, Agent Onsi?" Hamed quizzed, keeping his eyes on the thing.

"Perform a standard greeting to ascertain its level of sentience," the man answered on cue. It took a brief awkward silence for him to comprehend that Hamed meant him to perform the task. His mouth made a perfect "Oh!" as he hastily drew out a folded document. Opening it revealed a sepia-toned photo of his beaming face above a blue and gold Ministry seal. "Good morning, unknown being," he said in loud slow words, holding up his identification. "I am Agent Onsi and this is Agent Hamed of the Ministry of Alchemy, Enchantments, and Supernatural Entities. We hereby inform you that you are in breach of several regulations governing paranormal persons and sentient creatures, beginning with Article 273 of the criminal code which forbids trespass and inhabitation of public property owned by the State, Article 275 on acts of terrifying and intimidation of citizens . . ."

Hamed listened stupefied as the man rattled off a series of violations. He wasn't even certain when some of those had been put on the books.

" . . . and given the aforementioned charges," Onsi continued, "you are hereby instructed to vacate these premises and return to your place of origin, or, barring that, to accompany us to the Ministry for further questioning." Finishing, he turned with a satisfied nod.

Rookies, Hamed grumbled quietly. Before he could respond, a low moaning sounded in the car. There was little doubt where it came from, as the gray smoke had stopped its slithering and gone still.

"I think it understood me!" Onsi said eagerly.

Yes, Hamed thought dryly. *And you probably bored it to death. If it was already dead, you might have just bored it back to death.*

He was about say as much when there was a sudden terrible screeching.

Hamed moved to cover his ears at the sound, but was sent stumbling back as a jolt went through the tram. He might have fallen flat had he not reached out for one of the stanchions—catching the vertical pole by a hand. He looked up to see the gray smoke swirling furiously like an angry cloud, screaming as it swelled and grew. The lamps that lined the walls flickered rapidly and the tram began to tremble.

"Oh!" Onsi cried, trying to keep his footing. "Oh my!"

"Out! Out!" Hamed was yelling, already heading for the door. At one point, he slipped to a knee as the car shuddered hard and had to pick himself up—grabbing Onsi by the coat and pulling him along. When they reached the stairs something heavy pushed at them from behind, and they went tumbling down in tangle of flailing arms and legs until they were deposited unceremoniously onto the platform. From outside they could still hear the screeching as the hanging craft bucked and jumped. With a fury, the door slammed shut and all was quiet and still at once.

"I think," Hamed heard Onsi put in from where they lay in a heap, "we may confirm that Tram 015 is indeed haunted."

CHAPTER TWO

Late the next morning, Hamed found himself back with Onsi in the office of the Superintendent of Tram Safety & Maintenance at Ramses Station. Like before, the small space was hot, cramped, and filled with the constant resonance of a rattling fan that pushed out tepid air. There was also more sweet sudjukh, which somehow hadn't melted under the heat and remained tough as ever. He had to give his grudging respect to the candy's resiliency.

"So, it is not a ghost?" Superintendent Bashir was asking. His brow had wrinkled more and more as he listened to their report, until it now looked like crumpled parchment.

Hamed shook his head, working hard at a bit of sudjukh that was beyond chewing. At least this time they'd been offered some tea, and he washed the morsel down with the cool taste of hibiscus and mint. "I've investigated well over a dozen haunting cases and never seen a ghost," he answered. The fact was, in the Ministry's almost thirty years of operation, there'd been no evidence for the existence of ghosts—despite the growing number of spiritualists and self-proclaimed mediums that now flourished in the back alleys of Cairo's souks. Whatever became of the dead, it didn't appear they cared to converse with the living.

"Well, something is haunting the tram," the superintendent persisted. "You saw for yourself." He had the presence to look down at that, allowing Hamed to keep the embarrassment on his face to himself. It was still unseemly to remember how they'd been tossed about yesterday. Not the best look for the Ministry, and he was thankful his skin—the shade of harvested wheat—could not ever possibly show traces of red. Onsi, however, seemed wholly unbothered by the memory.

"Likely the tram is haunted by a djinn," he piped up, helping himself to a second glass of tea while secreting some sudjukh into a pocket.

The superintendent's eyebrows rose. "Djinn? In my tram? You're certain?"

"In these cases, it's almost always a djinn," Hamed replied.

Bashir seemed skeptical. "I've met djinn. Some work for the Transportation Bureau, as you expect. An earth Jann lives on my street. Several djinn, including a very old and powerful Marid, attend my masjid. That creature does not look like any djinn I've encountered. It is rather . . . small."

"Oh, there are more kinds of djinn than the Ministry

can even classify," Onsi countered quickly. "Just four centuries prior, the scholar al-Suyūṭī wrote of djinn that caused illnesses in the human mind and body. The early kalam on natural science held—"

"What Agent Onsi means to say," Hamed interjected, before they were led down a rumination on philosophical manuscripts, "is that djinn come in all sorts. So, it's quite possible for one to have taken over your tram."

"Well, what does it want?" Bashir asked.

"Hard to say," Hamed answered. "The djinn we're used to generally choose to interact and live among humans. There are others, Ifrit for instance, who we know keep their distance—most not even staying on this plane. Some we can't even communicate with. Those are often the haunting sort, lesser djinn beyond our classification. Likely, this one was drawn to the magic that operates your tram and has made its home there."

The superintendent sighed lengthily. "Djinn haunting my tram and attacking passengers." He finished with the hand gesture that accompanied the all-too-common Cairo slang: "Thank you, al-Jahiz."

It had been some forty years since the wandering Soudanese genius—or madman, take your pick—had, through a mix of alchemy and machines, bored a hole into the Kaf. The opening of the doorway to the otherrealm of the djinn had sent magic pouring out, changing the world forever. Now Cairenes evoked the disappeared mystic at every turn, his sobriquet uttered more often in mockery than praise to complain over the troubles of the age.

Hamed had never understood the phrase's ubiquity. Whether the Sufis were right, and al-Jahiz was indeed a herald of the Mahdi, or, as Copts feared, a sign of the apocalypse, seemed irrelevant. So too, he thought, were the continuing debates on whether al-Jahiz was the same as the medieval thinker of Basra, either traveled through time or reborn. Whatever the truth of it, without al-Jahiz there would be no Ministry. Egypt would not be one of the world's foremost powers. Indeed, the British might not even have been pushed out if not for the aid of the djinn. And those same djinn had built up Cairo to rival London or Paris. It often seemed that while the country proudly touted its modernity, it yet yearned wistfully for some simpler past.

"Al-Jahiz may have released more djinn upon the world," Onsi put in, as if reading Hamed's mind. "But it's hardly all his doing. Some number of djinn have always lived among us. They appear in too many of our oldest texts to believe otherwise: the *Kitab al-Fihrist,* the *Hamzanama,* and of course, the *Kitab al-Bulhan.* Why, it's commonly believed the old Khedive Muhammad Ali kept a secret djinn advisor, well over fifty years before al-

Jahiz arrived in Cairo. His victory over the Mamluks has even been credited to—"

"Before we wander down our national past," Hamed cut in once again—the man was like a stack of history books! "I think it's best I share our proposal for solving your problem." He untied the string holding together the leather folder he carried, and took out a sheet of paper, placing it on the desk and pushing it toward the superintendent. The man took it up and as he began to read, his eyebrows made a steady climb.

"Goodness!" he said at last, mopping at his temples. "This is quite detailed."

Hamed allowed a slight smile. He'd spent half the past day putting together the plan. Every element had been itemized with care. He was a bit proud. Even if the case was only a haunting.

"But this price," Bashir brooded. "So much?"

"Coaxing a djinn of unknown classification from your tram won't be easy," Hamed explained. "Much of the pricing you're seeing is the consultation fee for an elder djinn, a Marid who specializes in functioning as an intermediary. They're about the only class of djinn these entities will listen to. Besides that, we'll need to purchase some basic alchemical elixirs to purify the tram, in addition to a barrier spell—for safety you understand—and assorted other tools. We think that's the best way to assure the job is done effectively."

"It certainly is thorough," the superintendent admitted. "But I'm afraid it won't do."

Hamed's smile slid away. "What? Why? It's a very sound plan." He was somewhat offended. He knew well what he was about.

"Oh, I don't question your abilities, Agent Hamed," the superintendent said soothingly. "I mean this price. I simply can't pay it." Seeing Hamed's startled look he went on. "My office has limited expenditures for this sort of thing. The parliament is ever trying to find ways to cut our budget, yet demands we keep our systems running smoothly. Not to mention the Transportation Bureau is planning construction on several new lines to Heliopolis. There's just no money."

Hamed was at a loss. He hadn't anticipated that response. "I'm sorry," was all he could say. And he was. It was a very well-conceived and written-up plan. "I wish we could do more."

"Ah!" the superintendent exclaimed. "It's interesting you should say that." He reached into a desk drawer and drew out a sheet of paper of his own. "By chance, I was reading this interoffice memorandum on public safety earlier this morning. It was handed down several months ago from the national government and signed off by the Minister of the Interior. It deems any threat to the public good arising from mystical or preternatural occurrences a matter that falls under the jurisdiction of your agency."

Hamed took the paper from the man, trying not to snatch it as it was offered. By chance, was it? As if anyone went around reading months-old interoffice memoranda. A quick scan brought up brief memories of the Ministry lobbying for greater authority over public facilities. He thrust the paper over to Onsi, who took it and began reading in murmurs beneath his breath.

"I believe, since the haunting of the tram is now officially under your agency's dominion," Bashir stated delicately, "that any costs associated with its restoration to a less hazardous state should need come from your *own* funding." He paused in feigned uncertainty. "That is, if I have understood matters correctly?"

"I believe you have, superintendent," Onsi answered, finishing his read.

Hamed shot the younger man an annoyed look, but it was no use. He had gathered as much already. Somebody down at the Ministry hadn't anticipated this possible loophole. They certainly hadn't come across the likes of the wily Superintendent Bashir, either. The man put on a contrite smile that hid nothing before reaching for the bronze dish and offering it forward.

"More sweet sudjukh, Agent Hamed?"

~

Hamed trod heavily across the main floor of Ramses Station, indignation and humiliation knotted at the back of his head. Behind him, Onsi's shorter strides hurried to keep pace, weaving through the midday crowds. Around them sat Cairo's expansive transportation hub—a structure of glass and iron done up in the latest Neo-Pharaonic style. Gold-plated colonnades carved into bundles of papyrus lined the expansive hall, extending up to end in blossoming lotuses whose broad metal petals shifted and took on new shapes by the moment. The rows of columns supported a rotating ceiling of watery blue tiles that rippled like water, complete with swaying brass reeds timed to mechanical precision.

"I suppose," Onsi huffed, coming alongside, "we can take solace that you have secured a plan to solve the problem."

Hamed stopped and rounded on him. "Solving the problem isn't our problem," he snapped. "Paying for it is." He regretted it almost immediately. None of this was the younger man's fault. What a fine way to bring up a new investigator just raised from a cadet. "I mean," he started again, evening his voice, "the cost would eat through almost all of our discretionary budget."

Onsi mulled this over, pushing his spectacles further

onto a blunt nose. "Perhaps we could make do with what's left until our funds are replenished?" he suggested.

"That's months away," Hamed muttered. "The Ministry will just put us both on desk duty until then, so we can't run up any more expenses."

"Oh, that's dreadful!" Onsi said.

Quite dreadful. No one liked desk duty. It often seemed half their job was paperwork as it was. Who joined the Ministry for the thrill of filling out endless reports, in triplicate no less? Then again, he thought dismally, neither did they expect to spend their days haggling with government bureaucrats over haunted tram cars.

"We'll just have to find another way," he conceded, resigned to the prospect. He never got to say more as a sudden cry broke through the air—a high-pitched voice that was decidedly not the lilting chant of a muezzin. A few other passersby stopped at the sound, raising their hands up to each other in question and confusion.

"I believe it's coming from over there," Onsi suggested.

He had already begun to walk toward the commotion, and Hamed followed. They were approaching the center of the floor, toward a towering statue of the pharaoh for whom the station had been named. The colossal carving stood with hands at its side, right leg striding forward, and chiseled eyes of stone looking out with an eternal gaze. As they came closer the source of the cries could be seen plainly.

At the base of the statue was a group of women, some thirty or so. Many wore dresses reflecting modern Cairene or Parisian styles, while others were in more common loose seblehs. A few were veiled. At least two of their number were djinn—both female as well. Nearly all held signs and placards, listening as one of their number stood atop a ladder and spoke energetically.

"We meet today as a parliament!" she shouted. "A true parliament! Of women! We are half the nation! We helped found the nation! We represent its hopes and its despair! So long as we are not represented among those who vote for its leaders, the parliament of Egypt cannot be a true reflection of its people! We may have freed ourselves from foreign rule, but a nation cannot be liberated while its women are enchained!"

A great cry went up from the group, giving cheers and shouts in answer to her words.

Hamed accepted a leaflet from a young woman in a colorfully patterned hijab who couldn't have been more than eighteen. It featured a Janus-faced rendition of the pharaoh Hatshepsut: one side with the appearance of a mother holding a child and the other of a factory worker with tools. The words WE DEMAND THE VOTE! were printed in bold beneath.

"Ooh!" Onsi exclaimed, eyeing the handout. "Suffragettes! The bill on granting women the vote is being debated in parliament this week, I believe."

Who didn't know that, Hamed thought. It was on the front of every Cairo newspaper and the topic of debate in every coffee shop. Judging by the flyer, these women were part of the Egyptian Feminist Sisterhood—they had been pressing for reforms for over a decade now. They'd gotten more vocal in the past year, taking to the streets and public spaces. It was little wonder they'd chosen Ramses Station to protest. It was here, after all, that a young writer at the popular Egyptian magazine *La Modernité* had openly removed her veil back in 1899—causing a national sensation and revitalizing the movement.

"Do you think they'll actually get it?" Onsi asked. "The vote, I mean? In London, women can barely get a hearing in public on the issue."

Hamed shrugged. "Who can say?" He couldn't imagine Englishwomen anywhere near as bold as this. "They've managed to get the queen on their side, so that's in their favor." He watched as another woman rose to speak, this one veiled in a long Turkish-styled yashmak.

"Exciting times," Onsi remarked.

Perhaps too exciting for some, Hamed thought. More than a few faces in the station displayed shock at the scene. One old woman slapped her cheeks and her chest in dramatic fashion—muttering lamentations at the gathering.

Other bystanders shook their heads, a few men yelling angry words in parting. Most, however—especially the women, Hamed noticed—listened with interest. One way or the other, the country would see itself through this tumult, God willing.

"All this politics is making me hungry," he commented. "And we still have to figure out how to solve our case." He turned, gesturing to Onsi. "I know a place we can do both."

~

"My father's family is Coptic, from right here in Cairo," Onsi said. He absently ran a finger over the small black cross tattooed onto the inside of his right wrist, while nibbling away at a bit of sudjukh. He'd taken the superintendent up on his offer, making off with almost half the bowl, and had stashed it in his pockets.

"They live mostly in Shubra, and own a set of candy stores," he continued. That would explain the man's sweet tooth, Hamed assessed. "Now, my mother's family on her father's side are Copts as well, from down south in Minya—all cotton merchants. Made their wealth when the Americans had their troubles back in the sixties. Her mother, however, was a Nubian from Luxor. That produced quite the scandal, as this was before the religious tolerance laws. At any rate, this is all to say that of course

I love Nubian food! My grandmother prepared it for us on feast days—enough for me and all nine of my sisters."

Hamed sipped at his qasab, letting the cool sugarcane juice swirl around his tongue. That had to be the most roundabout way of getting to a point he'd ever witnessed. And did the man say *nine* sisters?

After departing Ramses Station, Onsi had waited while Hamed washed up and attended to prayer. They'd then made the short trip downtown to Makka, a Nubian restaurant of which Hamed was fond. The small eatery was styled to mimic a Nubian house: wooden yellow window frames, green-and-brown tiles on the floor, and sky-blue walls that matched the close-set tables and chairs. It wasn't like the upscale spots near the embassies, and you had to wind your way through some backstreets to find it. But the food was superb, and the mingled scents of cumin and garlic wafted through the air.

Onsi Youssef had been assigned to Hamed just this week, part of the Ministry's initiative to pair new re-cruits with seasoned agents. No doubt a barely con-cealed attempt to break the habits of investigators who generally preferred working alone. If they were going to be partners—the word still sounded odd to Hamed—it was probably advantageous to learn more about him than could be gleaned from his personnel record. Nothing like food and drink to loosen the

tongue. Though the man hardly needed encouragement.

"May I be so bold to ask, Agent Hamed," Onsi ventured, "after your family?"

Hamed shrugged. "All from Cairo, mostly in Bulaq now.
My father's a policeman. So are all three of my brothers. I
broke tradition. Graduated from the academy in the class of
'08."

Onsi's eyes lit up, and his smooth moon-shaped face
took on the look of a brown cherub. "1908? Isn't that
Agent Fatma's class? Do you know her well? She was the
talk of the academy!"

Hamed took another swallow of qasab. Of course she
was.

Agent Fatma el-Sha'arawi was something of a celebrity
in the Ministry. One of the few women agents, and quite
young. A peculiar sort, dressing in brash English suits.
Hamed didn't begrudge her that. But if she wanted to put
on men's clothing and stir up such a fuss, the Ministry offered perfectly reasonable uniforms.

"Yes, Agent Fatma and I attended the academy together," he answered. Not that they'd interacted all that
much. Just a few polite words here and there. Since grad-
uation, she'd gone on to become a Special Investigator,
solving high-profile cases that splashed across the front
pages of Cairo's dailies. Not that he begrudged her such

success either. She was a fine agent. There were some in the Ministry unsettled with a woman achieving such stature. But he prided himself on being a modern man, not given to outdated sentiments. Only, getting his photo in a newspaper, just once, would be nice.

"I hear she was the youngest recruit ever into the academy, at age twenty!" Onsi was going on. "We studied some of her cases." He leaned closer to whisper. "They're saying that the last one involved a set of rogue angels—perhaps dozens!"

Hamed put his cup down and fixed the younger man with a level stare. "We don't gossip about other agents' cases. And you'd do well to not spread Ministry hearsay." He had no idea why Agent Fatma's last case had been sealed, but these were precisely the kinds of ridiculous rumors such secrecy created. Those *things* were not angels, anyway.

Seeing Onsi's abashed look at the rebuke, he moved to change the subject. "So how did an Edwardian man like yourself end up at the Ministry? I understand you've been off at English boarding schools since thirteen."

Onsi perked up at that. "My family wanted me to have a *proper* education," he answered tactfully. Hamed didn't need to inquire as to his meaning. Egypt now boasted perhaps the best universities in the world. But some still insisted on sending their children off to England or France to learn, where blasphemous subjects like alchemy weren't on the curriculum. "It's all great nonsense," the man added hastily. "They're studying enchantments at the Sorbonne now. Both Oxford and Cambridge have opened up schools of the supernatural in the past two years. There's no ignoring the transcendental disciplines any longer."

No, Hamed thought wryly. Not after djinn and alchemy had routed the English at Tel El Kebir in '82. Then both the French and English at Sokoto in the nineties. Not to mention the disaster for the German-Italian Alliance at Adwa. Al-Jahiz hadn't just opened the Kaf of the djinn, he had made the walls to the supernatural realms porous across the globe, and the effects were still being felt. No surprise that the old empires had reversed their opinion on the "superstitions of the natives and Orientals."

"I longed to return to study in Cairo," Onsi continued dreamily. "So I left Oxford after my second year and enrolled at the university here, studying medieval manuscripts on esoteric sciences and thaumaturgical linguistics. I won over my family by arguing that the Ministry needed more Copts in its ranks, as they're always complaining about such inequities in civil society."

"That's a marked change from . . ." Hamed paused. "What is it you studied at Oxford?"

"The literature of the English playwrights." Onsi beamed. "I belonged to the Dramatic Society and played Katherina in our production of *The Taming of the Shrew*!"

Hamed was trying to reproduce that image when someone appeared at their table. He turned to find a tall young woman. Unmistakably Nubian, and striking, with curly black hair that peeked from beneath a yellow hijab. But what had him gaping like a fish was the rest of her clothing. She wore the common patterned Nubian dress, but the garment ended at her knees, held up at her shoulder by silver clasps. Beneath, she had on what looked like tight-fitting tan breeches, tucked into long leather boots. She stood there staring down at them expectantly.

"Good afternoon and peace be with you, madaam," he greeted her uncertainly.

"My, aren't we formal." The woman smirked. She squinted her dark eyes and tilted her head, causing her gold earrings to dangle. "Good afternoon and peace and health be with you as well."

Hamed was a bit taken aback. She was a bit off-putting for someone he didn't know. He didn't want Onsi getting the idea that he was the sort who kept unfamiliar women about.

"Madaam, am I acquainted with your father or brother?" he asked with care.

She chuckled throatily. "No, but I'm here to get acquainted with your order."

He then noticed she was holding a pad and pencil.

"I'm sorry. I didn't realize. I'm usually waited on by Uncle Tawfik."

"My grandaunt's oldest son," she replied. "I'm helping out at her restaurant while he's gone."

"Is he in good health?" Hamed asked. He always looked forward to the elder man, who called him Captain and was quick with a story or joke.

"Oh, he's fine," she answered. "Just visiting family down in Qena. Do you know what you want yet?"

Hamed faltered, as Tawfik usually brought out whatever was best. He said as much and she grinned back, tapping a finger to the tip of her nose: "In that case, I'll just have to do the same. Think I can manage." He eyed her dubiously, but accepted out of courteousness.

Some time later, he and Onsi sat quite sated, having gone through several bowls. The woman had been as good as her word, having plied them with roasted meats, salted fish, lentils, and stewed okra. At the moment, they were enjoying a tasty bread called kabed for dessert, which they ate with milk and honey. Much of the crowd had departed to sleep out Cairo's midday heat, and they had the place almost to themselves. Over their meal, they'd moved on to talking about the case but had so far gotten nowhere.

"We need a djinn, that's the short of it," Hamed said, rubbing wearily at his temples. "They're the only ones who'll be able to lure one of their kind from the tram. But no djinn will accept the paltry sum we're willing to offer." Djinn had taken to the modern world in every way, including demanding proper wages. Many were even unionized. Their abilities didn't come cheap.

"Perhaps," Onsi ventured carefully, "we can persuade a djinn with something other than money? I understand there are a few who still grant wishes—"

Hamed cut him off with a stiff shake of his head. "Never seek a wish from a djinn. They're much better at negotiating than we are and things almost always go badly." Wish-granting hazards accounted for at least a fifth of the Ministry's yearly case load, and he'd seen more than his share.

The two were sitting back, quiet and bereft of ideas, when someone pulled a chair up to their table. Hamed started in surprise to find it was the bold young woman again. She'd taken off her server's apron, which now hung casually over a shoulder.

"You will forgive me for disturbing your meal," she said with a placating gesture. "But I couldn't help but overhear your troubles—something about a haunted carriage or trolley?" Hamed glared indignantly but her tone only turned sharp. "Oh, stop tightening up that great big square jaw of yours. The place is nearly empty and you two have been going at this for almost an hour.

You know how boring serving food is? What else am I to do to pass the time? Speak with lower voices if you don't want me to listen! Besides, you're not the first of the Ministry's Spooky Boys to come in here, you know."

Hamed felt self-consciously at his jaw. It wasn't so square. And Spooky Boys?

"As I was saying," she went on in a calmer voice. "I think you're going about this all the wrong way. Djinn aren't the only ones who can coax out this spirit. There are cheaper solutions. Not as fancy as all your alchemy and enchantments, but have you considered a Zār ritual?"

Hamed was set to explain that Ministry Agents didn't go around using folk remedies for sensitive cases. But his mouth wouldn't work. Because astonishingly, she had a good point.

"Zār?" Onsi asked, for once not in the know.

"A ceremony," Hamed muttered, turning the idea over in his head. "It's held to cure ailments caused by lesser djinn. The Ministry considers it too disorganized and scattered to classify as a true discipline." At this the woman made a disagreeable sound. "But I think it could just work."

"I can give you a name and an address," she offered. Ripping a page from her pad, she scribbled hastily and pushed it forward. "But you'll have to convince them to take you on. I'm sure you Spooky Boys can handle that."

Hamed palmed his chest, tipping his head. "Thank you, very much, madaam."

She smiled back. "My pleasure." Standing, she teasingly pressed a finger beneath each eyelid—then ruined the gesture with an off-putting wink.

"She was helpful," Onsi put in, watching her stride away in those odd boots.

"Perhaps," Hamed answered, his mind already working. "Finish up. We need to make an appointment with a sheikha."

CHAPTER THREE

The address on the slip of paper took them along Sha'ib El Banat. It had previously been Soliman Street, named for a French military commander under one of the old pashas. Now it carried the name of the djinn builder who had transformed modern Cairo into an industrial capital. It was also the name of a mountain range somewhere in the eastern desert, as djinn never gave their real names and used such places as monikers instead.

Hamed had expected to end up in a back alley somewhere, and not along one of the most well-known commercial centers in the city—with tall buildings reflecting a mixture of architectural styles. They stopped at a corner, before a building with a rounded front and multiple floors each supported by Corinthian columns. At the apex, a carved relief depicted pharaohs upon thrones beneath a roof capped by a white dome.

"Here we are," he told Onsi, matching up the address. "Just as our helpful server suggested. Tell me, what did you notice about her?"

Onsi pursed his lips, mulling over the unexpected

question. "She appears about my age, I suppose. Much prettier, certainly. And, there are the pants and boots. An interesting woman."

That she certainly was, Hamed agreed. "What did you notice about her earrings?"

Onsi scrunched up his face in recollection. "Earrings? They were gold. In the likeness of an animal of some kind? Perhaps a bird?"

"A cow," Hamed corrected. "A golden cow, with a disc between its horns. An emblem of the goddess Hathor."

The younger man's eyes widened. "An idolater!"

"They don't exactly call themselves that," Hamed pointed out. The entrance of djinn and magic into the world had changed society in some unanticipated ways. It had even sent a few seeking after Egypt's eldest gods, whose temples and statues had remained stubbornly steadfast through time. There were probably dozens of such cults in Cairo alone. Most remained underground, as even the vaunted new religious tolerance laws offered their adherents little protection.

"Not surprising that she knows where to find practitioners of a Zār," he continued, walking up to pull at a door latch. "Always keep your eyes sharp, Agent Onsi. Sometimes what you least expect is staring right at you." His words died on his tongue as the door opened.

He had expected a reception area, but was greeted instead by a foyer filled with women. Dozens of women. They all chatted loudly, so busily moving to and fro that most scarcely bothered to pay the two men any mind. Hamed surveyed the walls about them, which were plastered with artwork. One featured a veiled woman with arms outstretched that read: ARISE YE WOMEN! Another a young factory girl, sitting at a loom machine with the slogan: WOMEN ARE AWAKENING! A third portrayed a woman in modern dress: EGYPT, FREE YOUR WOMEN!

His gaze traveled up a stone staircase to where a large half-moon banner hung from a balcony, displaying the familiar double-faced Hatshepsut upon a red and green background, the words *Egyptian Feminist Sisterhood Office #3* inscribed across the top in golden script. He was still putting the pieces of this unexpected scene together as a figure moved to block his vision: a woman in all black, her face set into a sour expression.

"There you are!" she exclaimed without any greeting. "It's been two full hours! Do we ask so much of you to arrive when you say you will?" He opened his mouth in protest, but the woman snapped her head upward and clicked her tongue, cutting off whatever he was going to say. "I don't want to hear your excuses. You should be ashamed to do business as you do! Where is your self-respect and how do you expect others to have it for you?"

Hamed had taken an involuntary step back under the harangue, and he saw Onsi do the same. The woman was sturdily built and old enough to be his mother. In fact, she spoke to him as if she *was* his mother. She clutched her head in clear exasperation. "See here how many more of these we have to produce! If you don't fix the machine soon we won't have enough for the rallies planned before the vote!" He followed her gesture, only now noticing the leaflets that the other women were gathering into neat stacks against the walls. They all read: WE DEMAND THE VOTE!

Finding his wits, he finally spoke up. "Madaam, we aren't here to fix your machine."

She glared at him. "Then who will fix it? You expect one of us to?"

He hastily dug out his identification and brandished it like a shield. "I'm Agent Hamed and this is Agent Onsi. We're with the Ministry of Alchemy, Enchantments, and Supernatural Entities."

The woman peered closely at his photo and the official seal bearing his name. She scowled beneath a set of thick eyebrows. "But we didn't call you. We need a machinist for the printer. Why would they send us the Ministry?"

"Madaam, no one called us," Hamed explained. This was becoming tedious. "We don't know anything about your printer or your work. We came looking for a sheikha, and didn't realize this was one of the Sisterhood's headquarters. Perhaps we've been misled. If so, we apologize for troubling your house."

The woman eyed them both, drawing up her shawl, then said almost dismissively, "You want Nadiyaa. She rents an office seven stairs up. The green door. We have the lift busy, so you'll have to take the stairs." She left as hurriedly as she had appeared, likely to find her errant machinist.

Hamed and Onsi exchanged wrung-out looks before crossing the floor through the crowd to begin the long climb up. On each floor they passed, there were more women engaged in work. Making signs, drafting petitions, even teaching chants. If there was to be a vote on the suffrage bill this week, he could understand their urgency. He noticed that among the obvious Cairenes there were also rural women from the countryside, recognizable in their simple but elaborately wrapped gallabiyahs. It seemed the Sisterhood had brought in members from all over for their rallies—a prudent move, as the early movement had struggled to make itself inclusive of more than just the urban classes.

By the time they reached the seventh floor, Hamed found he was laboring for breath. Onsi wasn't faring much better. They stopped to rest near a great mural depicting crowds of men with djinn hidden among them.

In the middle, atop a carriage, were three women, all in black dress and long white veils, one of them standing and appearing to speak.

"*The Women of '79,*" Onsi remarked, naming the famous painting. This was of course only a replica. The much larger original sat at the art museum in Gezira, a dedication to the women who had taken part in the 1879 nationalist uprising against the British. Not surprising. Women, after all, had been some of al-Jahiz's more dedicated followers. Looking past the mural, his eyes landed on a dark green door at the end of the hall.

"I think that's where we're meant to be," he deduced. They walked up, and this time rapped once before opening it slowly. Inside they found two seated women working a wide brass-faced switchboard, hands moving rapidly as they spoke into headphones and plugged long black cords into copper-plated jacks.

"Good afternoon, sirs, may I be of help?" a voice slurred.

Hamed turned to another woman behind a wide black painted desk that stood on animal-shaped legs. Not a woman, he corrected, but a djinn. Her skin was a deep shade of red, the color of a dark ruby, even to her lips. A set of corded silver horns replaced hair, flowing past her shoulders and matching decorated fingernails that were long as talons. She was also, very possibly, the most beautiful being he had ever seen, with depthless eyes that sparkled like gems in moonlight. His mouth went dry at the sight of her, but he managed to stammer out a greeting and show his identification, asking after her mistress.

"Please have a seat, agents," she answered in that slurring tone. "I'll inquire whether the sheikha has a moment to meet with you. Would you care for some drink? Tea perhaps?"

Hamed nodded dreamily, giving his thanks. His nostrils were filled with a miasma of scents that carried from the djinn: jasmine, honey, and pungent cinnamon, to name a few—so strong he could taste them on his tongue. She gave a demure smile as she rose to go, standing a good foot above him. And he couldn't help but notice that even in her long maroon dress she walked with a gait that was almost hypnotic.

"Quite a remarkable djinn," Onsi commented breathlessly as they sat.

Hamed didn't answer, still trying to clear the haze that tickled his senses. He instead took to watching the two women at the switchboard. Now that he listened close, he could hear they were taking what appeared to be orders—for people seeking the Zār. From what he made out, the calls were coming in from all over Cairo.

The callers were all women, beseeching ceremonies for every manner of thing: fever sickness, childlessness, depression, addiction, ill fortune. The list was endless, and the two operators were forced to keep up a busy pace. It was a stunning revelation, and he wondered how many thoroughly modern Cairene women were in the privacy of their homes participating in what was often publicly dismissed as backward superstition. The Ministry had obviously grossly underestimated the ceremony's popularity.

"Agents, the sheikha will see you now," that slurred voice came.

Hamed looked up to find a tall male djinn standing over him in maroon robes. He was as ruby-skinned as the female djinn, and had those same long silver horns that curved down his back like hair. A relation perhaps? That strong scent carried with him, too. And his black eyes held a familiar sparkle. Hamed blinked as it struck him. Why, this wasn't another djinn, it was the same one! He stared openly, unable to catch himself, and the djinn put on a smile that was more knowing than demure.

"Your tea, agents? And if you'll come with me."

Hamed accepted his glass, offering the other to Onsi as they rose to follow.

"I've heard of this class of djinn!" the younger man leaned in to whisper. "I wonder how they prefer to be addressed? Still remarkably beautiful!"

And with that same mesmerizing walk, Hamed had to

admit. They were led through another door to a small room. The djinn bid them sit and left them there, closing the door behind.

The two figures before them now were as different as could be. The first was not a woman at all, nor a djinn, but a boilerplate eunuch. Only it was of a design of which Hamed was unfamiliar. All the machine-men he'd ever encountered lacked specific anatomical features, composed of barrel-shaped torsos attached to jointed limbs. This model was decidedly not a machine-man, but instead a machine-woman: the light curves of its lithe body easily perceptible even beneath long white robes. Where boilerplate eunuchs were uniformly featureless, this one displayed a brass face carved like a statue of some ancient goddess, the light from a lamp reflecting a metallic glare off a set of prominent cheekbones. The peculiar automaton stood inert, hands folded at its middle, looking out at them from behind blank oval-shaped eyes, full lips engraved into the barest smile.

The other figure was unmistakably human, a woman in her middle years with braided hair the tint of gray ash. She sat behind a polished sandalwood desk etched throughout with interlocking circles of Sufi symbology, including a calligraphic sigil commonly used to denote al-Jahiz. That was no surprise, as the woman was Soudanese, obvious by the indigo thoub that wrapped her from ankle to head. There was a glaring red, black, and green tri-color pennant bearing a white crescent moon and spear spread out on the wall behind—the flag of the Mahdist Revolutionary People's Republic.

Hamed greeted the sheikha, introducing both himself and Onsi. She met this with cool civility, her brown eyes inspecting them as one would a pair of vipers who'd invited themselves to your dinner table. Her fingers absently traced the intricate henna patterns that covered her other hand as they exchanged pleasantries, and he wondered what so disquieted her about their presence. He wasn't kept wanting for an answer long.

"I expected the Ministry to make its way to my door sooner or later," she commented in the clear accents of her home country. "But I think you must know that I cannot aid you in your endeavor." Agent Hamed looked at her, startled. He hadn't even made his request. Misreading his confusion, her already flat stare tightened to steel. "I won't bow to any coercion to make me register with the Ministry. And I will tell you now, every other sheikha or kodia will resist such attempts as well—not when it means exposing women to misguided men who label what we do some baladi custom or even haram!"

It took a moment for him to take her meaning and he chided himself for his thoughtlessness. Of course she would think that two agents unexpectedly appearing at her office were here to bring the Zār under Ministry control. Given what he knew of the ceremony—with its numerous leaders and small cells—there were likely hundreds of such women throughout the city. She was probably also right. Once the Ministry learned of the extensive nature of their operations, there'd be calls for registering and sanctioning their practices. But at least he could assure her that wasn't their current purpose.

"Sheikha Nadiyaa," he rejoined respectfully, "I regret if we've caused you undue worry. But we haven't come here to do any such thing." At least not today, he reflected guiltily. "We're here seeking your help, if you'll give it." She fixed him with a disbelieving look, and he hurriedly explained what they were after. She sat listening, her expression impenetrable. When he finished she said nothing right away, still carefully digesting his words. At the least, her fingers had ceased their tracing.

"I must confess, Agent Hamed," she said at last, "this is not at all what I expected." Her shoulders relaxed, more at ease as she sat back in her chair. And she took up a glass of red tea that had sat untouched. "You tell quite a story, with this possessed tram car. I have never heard of such a thing. But tell me, why haven't you sought the aid of one of the greater djinn?" Hamed felt his moustache twitch as he grasped for a tactful reply. "Ah," she sighed, reading his hesitation, "you suppose a sheikha comes cheaper than the rates of some high-priced Marid. Well you're right. We aren't trying to make wealth off the women of the city, though we ask that each give according to their kind. Unfortunately, however, I will have to disappoint you by denying your request."

Hamed felt the wind collapse beneath his hopes. "But why?" he asked.

The sheikha took a long draught of tea before answering. "First, you misunderstand what it is we do. The Zār is not a ceremony to drive out spirits. We assess each woman to understand the nature of her affliction. It could be that the possessing djinn has been stirred by the woman's actions or some disruptive presence. Maybe it wants something. Or brings warning. Some are just fickle. Whatever the matter may be, we work to appease the djinn, to bring the person more in harmony with the spirit so that its wants may be pacified. We are not exorcists." She bit off the last word with clear disdain, taking another sip of tea as if to wash away its taste. "So, as you see, there is nothing we can do for your tram, which is not truly a person. And we are not in the habit of forcing djinn from where they choose to reside."

Well, that wasn't encouraging. Hamed mentally ran through what he knew of the Zār, which was admittedly little. The tradition was believed to have come from Abyssinia, practiced by Christians and Muslims alike. It had traveled throughout the horn then up the Nile into Soudan, Egypt, spreading beyond into the Maghreb. It was the domain of women, or at least he'd never heard of a man leading a Zār. As he understood, they dealt with lesser djinn, the kind that caused troubles and who rarely even took corporeal form. How anyone could appease such creatures was beyond him. He was wondering how to break their impasse when Onsi stepped into the awkward silence.

"Sheikha Nadiyaa," he asked, "have you ever ridden on a tram?"

She shook her head, her face contorting. "Watching them speed along above me is dizzying enough. I appreciate the wonders of this age, but I prefer the earth firmly beneath my feet."

"Well, that may explain your misapprehension of the matter," Onsi replied. "Excuse me for my disagreement, sheikha, but I'm not certain the differentiation you are making between a possessed person and this tram is warranted."

"Oh?" she asked, raising an appraising eyebrow. "Please enlighten me."

The man seemed eager to do so. "The tram in question is a design of the djinn," he explained. "It is endowed with a machine mind imbued with magic. The tram is thus capable of thought, which it uses to guide itself and its passengers safely. Those dizzying feats you witness are decisions made by a thinking being. Given that, I submit the tram is little different from a person who suffers an affliction and needs your help. Did not the earliest Sufi masters write that to practice generosity was foremost in achieving spiritual perfection?"

Both of the woman's eyebrows were raised now, as were Hamed's. "I am curious to know how a Copt is versed with the concept of futuwwa," she said, glancing to his tattooed wrist. "You make an intriguing supposition. However, your argument only leads to another trouble. If these trams are thinking beings, as you say, then they exist in a state of slavery. And I will not aid in such an exploitative system."

"Slavery!" Hamed exclaimed, thoroughly perplexed. "How does slavery enter into this?"

The sheikha drew herself up, and when she spoke it was with the practice of rote recitation. "Thinking beings, whether wrought by God or man, should not be bound to serve but have the right of choosing their lot. In the People's Republic, all forms of bondage have been done away with. No man or woman may hold another as property. Neither do we allow sentient tram cars or machinemen made in our likeness to toil to our whims while we profit from their labor. Al-Jahiz himself, as you know, was a slave soldier to one of your pashas. He spoke often on the harm that enslavement does to the souls of those bound by the chain, and the souls of those who wield it. Many djinn would tell you as much, for they abhor slavery perhaps greater than all other earthly vice."

Hamed was somewhat familiar with that history. Slavery had been abolished with the birth of an independent Egypt back in '83. In Soudan, however, the early Mahdist movement had sought to revive the practice—until a djinn converted its leadership to Revolutionary Sufism. Still, Hamed could not help to mention the obvious which was only feet away.

"Sheikha Nadiyaa. I mean no discourtesy, but you yourself are the owner of a boilerplate eunuch."

The sheikha turned to the machine-woman who had stood immobile all this time. "Agent Hamed, you again misunderstand. I don't own a boilerplate eunuch. Fahima is not my property, but my assistant. Isn't that so, Fahima?"

"Yes, Madaam," the boilerplate eunuch affirmed. "I believe the agent has mistaken the nature of our relationship."

Hamed almost fell out of his chair. That boilerplate eunuch had spoken! Her lips hadn't moved, and her face remained as unchanged as a statue. But those had been her words! And not just the usual "Yes" or "No" or "How may I serve?" but a complex sentence!

"Fahima is a liberated machine," the sheikha said, not

bothering to hide her amusement at his flummoxed look. "She was a common boilerplate eunuch once, but I helped her see she was more. She began thinking for herself. Soon she chose to become the person you see now. She's not the only one, either. There are others of her kind, and they are bringing their comrades to consciousness. You are looking at the future."

Hamed still couldn't stop gaping. Boilerplate eunuchs becoming people? He could already envision the chaos, as machine-men began confronting their owners, demanding wages or work they preferred. If the woman had any such concerns, it was lost behind her self-satisfied expression. You let some people read Marx . . .

"The sheikha is perhaps optimistic," Fahima put in, tilting her head slightly. "Only a few of my kind share the innate spark to become more. Perhaps it was our particular design. Or some science we do not yet understand. Most are content with their work, and when pressed want little more than perhaps a day to themselves, or two."

Is that all? Hamed thought sardonically.

"I don't know that this changes anything," Onsi interjected, appearing to have put together an argument. "Whether thinking machines can be enslaved or not makes for fascinating discourse. However, this seems a poor reason to allow Tram 015 to languish in misery. You would no more be aiding in its enslavement by curing its affliction than you would in healing an exploited laborer. The state of the distressed doesn't negate your ethical obligation."

The sheikha seemed taken by his words, and she looked on consideringly. Onsi pressed the opening with the skill of a chess player. "Besides, one can imagine that such an act of kindness would make Tram 015 more receptive to your message of freedom." That made her sit up with interest. Hamed whipped his head to glare at the man. They weren't here to start a revolution!

"What do you think of the agent's reasoning, Fahima?" the sheikha inquired.

"I believe it has merit," the machine-woman replied.

Sheikha Nadiyaa nodded her agreement. "I would very much like to talk proletarian dialogues and the philosophies of Sufi masters and Coptic thinkers with you one day, Agent Onsi."

"Oh!" the man exclaimed, beaming. "I would like that very much!"

"Agent Hamed," she addressed him sharply. "I'll see what I can do for your tram."

"Thank you!" he said gratefully. Though a part of him was still trying to figure out what had just happened.

"Now," she said sternly. "Let's talk about what you can give."

They spent the next half of an hour listening as the sheikha put together a plan and rattled off fees. Fahima stood by dutifully with a hand-held mechanical calculator. Her tactile metal fingers moved in a blur, punching at the numbered keys that clacked as the adding machine churned out a spool of printed paper. When it was done, they presented Hamed with the lengthy bill.

He almost choked on his tea.

CHAPTER FOUR

The next morning, Agent Hamed found himself standing outside Tram 015 at the aerial yard above Ramses Station. He had managed to get Sheikha Nadiyaa to take up the matter immediately, rather than placing them on her busy schedule—in which case she might not have attended to the tram until next Mawlid. It had cost him extra, of course. There seemed to be a fee for everything! She claimed she was only being fair, making them meet in kind what she did every petitioner. Still, it was yet far cheaper than soliciting the aid of a high-priced djinn. Besides, this Zār came with one of its own.

He looked to the ruby-skinned djinn—at present a woman—who was helping prepare the tram for the ceremony. It turned out the djinn was more than just a secretary. "Jizzu has been with my family for generations," the sheikha had informed him. "Long before al-Jahiz, we accepted without question that djinn lived and worked among us. The ritual I perform today has come out of that bond."

Some kind of personal djinn, Hamed suspected. Perhaps even a Qareen. There were only a few such cases recorded by the Ministry—djinn like Jizzu who attached themselves directly to persons, whole families, or lineages, sometimes even counted among them. He would have to remember to jot this down in his report. That was, provided this plan worked out at all.

"I pray it goes well," Onsi had replied, when Hamed shared as much. He spoke through bites of sweet sudjukh, having replenished his stores of the candy from Bashir's dish that morning. The superintendent had looked on in growing bafflement as Sheikha Nadiyaa and her retinue filed into his small office, all holding bundles and various items—from candles to foodstuffs, even several live chickens. By the time Jizzu and Fahima appeared, Bashir couldn't decide if he wanted more to stare at the captivatingly attractive djinn or the enunciating boilerplate eunuch.

"God willing," Hamed intoned in answer. He watched as the women draped parts of the tram with white cloth. "What is it they're doing now?"

"I spent the night reading on the ritual," Onsi related. "Do you know, the Zār is very different depending on the region? Even some clans living in close proximity in Soudan practice it different from one another. And Christians different from Muslims, though at times it is practiced together. I believe what they are doing now is preparing the patient. Ordinarily this would be a woman placed into white robes. Ah yes, see there? Now they are applying the kohl beneath the eyes."

Hamed could see the women were now indeed using brushes to paint the black cosmetic beneath the two bulbous lanterns of the tram. It seemed Onsi had impressed the sheikha enough with his argument to have her treat the car as an actual person. Remembering all that talk of "liberating" Cairo's machines, he hoped they wouldn't regret putting the radical notion into her head.

"This will be quite a thing to witness," Onsi remarked. "Is Superintendent Bashir certain he doesn't want to see?"

"Quite certain," Hamed drolled. The man had been so put off by the idea of the ritual—and the prospect of encountering the djinn haunting his tram car—that he'd made some excuse of work duties, leaving them to their own devices.

"Agents!" Nadiyaa called. "We'll need your help here."

Hamed walked over with Onsi. He hoped the women only needed him to carry things. He'd been eyeing the cages of chickens dubiously. As he understood, the Zār had to end in a sacrifice. He wasn't averse to such things, but the blood and feathers were likely to get onto his uniform. And he'd just had it cleaned and pressed. But when they got closer, he saw that she held out two round flat Tar drums.

"The Zār is always accompanied by music," she told them. "Ordinarily I would hire a troupe of men to play. But with such short notice, none were readily available. We will have to make do with what we can. And you will help. Now find your places, we're set to begin."

Hamed took the broad drum hesitantly. He hadn't even known men were allowed into the Zār, and hadn't expected he'd be called on to participate. But there was no time to object, as they were quickly hustled among the group of women. A few of them were Nadiyaa's age, but most were younger—with faces that reflected the variety of Soudan, Egypt, perhaps even Abyssinia. All were dressed in patterned dresses and hijab, in contrast with the simple white they'd hung about the tram. The two men were hurried into bright blue gallabiyahs over their uniforms—colors, they were told, the djinn might find pleasing.

In moments, the strumming strings of an oud and the fluty resonance of several reed neys played in the morning air. The sounds emanated from Fahima, who seemed to make them as easily as Hamed could whistle. The machine-woman walked alongside Nadiyaa in the front, flanking the sheikha's left as Jizzu took her right. An odd enough trio, he judged, as he began to slap a palm on the goatskin hide of the Tar drum.

"You there, the tall broad one!" a woman behind him called. "We're trying to appease the djinn, not drive it off! Try to catch the beat. You keep rhythm like an Englishman!"

There were some titters at this and Hamed felt his face flush. He did *not* keep rhythm like an Englishman! It was only that it was hard just starting out. And all the different sounds were a bit confusing. He cast a glance over to Onsi—who was pounding away on his drum at a hearty pace, moving in perfect time to the music. A few of the women offered him compliments and Hamed gritted his teeth. He was being shown up by someone who had gone to school at Oxford? He renewed his efforts as the door to the tram was opened. They had to enter single-file through the narrow passage, and by the time Hamed made his way up the steps, the car was already filled with people.

It had that same feel as before—the air thick, cold, and heavy. Nadiyaa and Jizzu stood off at one end while he and the other women occupied another. A round wooden tray had been placed on a three-legged stool in the center of the car. It was covered in white cloth, but beneath could be made out heaps of nuts and dried fruits. Nearby sat the cages of chickens—an altar of offerings to the djinn. The already dim space fast filled with incense smoke billowing from two coffers that could be seen under the flickering lamps. The pungent smell of frankincense soon filled the air. It all mixed with the drums, Fahima's music, and a steady chanting led by the sheikha and the other women, creating a heady atmosphere.

Hamed squinted through the haze to the clockwork mass in the tram's ceiling, searching for the spirit. He found it almost immediately—that sinuous tendril of gray smoke that slithered among the turning gears. It appeared to take notice of the visitors and ceased its constant movement. Going still, it sat there in one place and he couldn't help shake an eerie feeling of being watched.

His attention was drawn to Nadiyaa, who had begun the ceremony in earnest. She was singing loudly, her voice carrying a piercing cry, calling out her name and speaking to the spirit directly. Then, she began to dance.

Hamed had been told of this part of the ritual. Before a spirit could be reasoned with and appeased, it had to be identified. In a way, the Ministry observed similar rules. Only where he used classification charts, the sheikha used dance—quick circular whirls that made her garments spin like a dervish.

Every class of djinn the Zār dealt with was said to have its own particular song and rhythm. As she danced each in turn, she kept an unwavering eye on the hovering spirit above, gauging its reaction. At her side, Jizzu moved in harmony. The djinn had shifted to a male form, and now spun beside Nadiyaa with a fluid grace. This must be what it meant, he now realized, for a sheikha to dance with her djinn. The two seemed to enter a trance, becoming one graceful being as they sought to commune with the unknown djinn. Had he put on his spectral goggles, Hamed would not have been surprised to see waves of magic churning about them. He could feel it even here, washing over him and setting the fine hairs along his skin to standing.

In his own circle, where the other women danced and tossed their hair about, Hamed kept his eyes and wits sharp. Nadiyaa had proven stubbornly reluctant about forcing the djinn to leave the tram. But through Onsi's philosophical wrangling, they'd managed to convince her that she might appeal to the spirit to find a host more amenable to its wants. Despite all that business about sentient machines, he couldn't fathom why any djinn would want to spend years possessing a tram car. Maybe the thing just didn't know where it was.

A sudden commotion caught his attention. The spirit had become active again, mimicking Nadiyaa and Jizzu, trying to match their movements. As it did so, it also began to grow, becoming bigger by the moment. No, not just grow, Hamed realized—it was taking form! They had been told about this beforehand. The djinn might choose to reveal itself when ready to make contact, perhaps even becoming corporeal. It was working! Slowly he watched as what had once been an obscure mass coalesced into a more definable shape. It took on aspects of a head, then added a torso with arms and legs until reaching what it desired.

Hamed stared in surprise. The djinn he knew could take on any shape. Some had the heads of beasts or fantastic creatures. Others, like Jizzu, seemed like more majestic versions of humans—taller, stronger, or abnormally beautiful. This djinn didn't look like any of those. It instead looked nothing more than a girl.

A ghostly girl, certainly, whose moon-pale skin carried an ethereal gray cast, almost glowing amid the gloom and incense smoke. She was thin. Not the type of thin that looked starved, but instead delicate—as if she were made of something that might shatter if touched. Her eyes were overly large, with pitch black liquid pupils set into a pale gray face with a small nose and even smaller lips tinged in blue—the only color on her. A bone-white dress covered her like a slip down to her ankles, where her bare feet showed. She hovered horizontally above them, staring down with her bold eyes while long strands of slivery hair flowed about as if she were submerged in water.

Nadiyaa had stopped both her dance and song. She took guarded steps forward, looking up at the spirit, speaking and offering her name. The ghostly girl tilted her head curiously, then answered back. Hamed listened close to her speech. Her voice had the same grating quality as the screech that had driven him and Onsi from the tram on their first visit. This time it wasn't nearly as bad, as she was speaking, not screaming. But he still couldn't make her out. What language was that? By the look on Nadiyaa's face, she was equally puzzled. She seemed set to try again when the girl unexpectedly pounced.

It happened so fast, Hamed wasn't certain what he'd seen. The spirit had lunged for the sheikha, only it wasn't the girl. At least not any more. In a blur, it had changed once again, this time into something horrifying. The young girl's face became ancient, shriveled and decayed like the mummified dead that lay buried deep in Egypt's oldest tombs. Her long silvery hair turned wan, and now hung in uneven and tangled tresses. The rest of her body had grown and elongated, becoming tall and monstrous. Narrow arms jutted from hulking shoulders, stretching to the knee and ending in long fingers of sharpened bone.

The hag opened her mouth and let out that familiar screech, so that the other women clutched at their ears in pain. Nadiyaa had gone down under the attack, and the spirit raised one of those deadly arms to slash. Hamed already had his pistol out—though he had no idea what bullets would do against such a thing. But Jizzu was there first, taking on a form that looked like the man and woman at once. They moved to stand protectively over Nadiyaa, baring sharp ivory teeth in threat as the ruby in their eyes burned fierce. The hag gave another great screech, realizing there was easier prey, and turned abruptly on the car's other inhabitants.

Hamed took aim as the spirit came and jumped out in front. He never got off a shot as she batted him aside without stopping. He went tumbling at the strong blow, sliding across the tram floor to knock over the altar, where terrified chickens flapped and squawked noisily in their cages. He didn't stop until slamming up against a bolted down chair, losing his tarboosh along the way. He watched helplessly as the spirit fell upon the gathered women, scattering them like dolls. There were stomach-turning screams as those claws slashed away, adding the sounds of tearing cloth to the air.

Somehow Fahima managed to get herself between them, standing with arms flung wide. The spirit tore at her dress, ripping the front to shreds. As if angered at finding brass beneath rather than flesh, the hag raked the machine-woman's metal torso—throwing off showering sparks to light up the dim gloom of incense smoke. Those claws might have reduced the machine-woman to shrapnel if not for a voice that boomed through the car to draw everyone's attention.

Nadiyaa was standing. Her face was awash with fury,

and she was chanting at the top of her lungs. The spirit twisted her neck unnaturally, fixing the sheikha with emptied eye sockets, and opened a mouth crammed full of jagged teeth to let fly a string of words in its unknown language. Hamed didn't need to understand to know the things were curses. The foul magic that clung to them sent up a deathly sour stench, and he gagged reflexively.

But where the curses struck, hair-thin golden lines of Sufi geometric symbols could be seen, infusing the air about the sheikha like a ward of light. She remained steadfast, chanting and pushing forward. Soon the spirit was in retreat and howling in rage. The hag's arms began to shrink and her whole body collapsed in on itself until once again there was only a small trail of gray smoke. Retreating back to the clockwork brain in the tram's ceiling, the spirit played out its anger—setting the car to tremble and quake.

Hamed didn't waste time. He ran to help several of the women up, pausing only to snatch up his tarboosh. Onsi was doing the same, escorting them quickly to the door. In ones and twos, they filed out of the tram and onto the safety of the platform. Outside, everyone watched as the car shook wildly. There was a sudden lapse of silence—before a mass of blood, feathers, and gore came flying out the door. What was left of the altar and the chickens was now mangled and reduced to pulp. With a slam, the door to the tram shut and all went quiet.

Releasing a long-held breath, Hamed tried to get his bearings—still dazed at what had just happened. He hastily counted over the women to see that everyone was there. Miraculously, none of them had been seriously hurt. The front of their clothes had been torn terribly, but those bony claws hadn't broken the skin. Fahima was another matter. Deep gashes, rent across the machine-woman's middle, even now leaked bits of steam and fluid. Nadiyaa knelt, tending to her with evident worry. When she was done, she stood and stalked toward the men.

Hamed almost backed away at sight of the storm cloud churning in her face, but instead asked: "Will she be all right?"

Nadiyaa gave a curt nod. "Yes. Praise be to God, she is strongly made. A machinist will have to repair her wounds and rebuild what was broken."

"What happened? Why did the spirit attack you?"

"I don't know," she answered, her voice heating. "I only know one thing—that is no djinn! I went through all seven classes of lesser djinn spirits that are known to the Zār, and that *thing* belongs to none of them. Your tram is haunted by some foreign, unknown spirit. But don't call it a djinn!"

Hamed listened, dumbfounded. Not a djinn? A foreign spirit? "But from where?" he asked.

"I don't know that either," the sheikha replied. "It spoke in some other tongue, a dialect of Turkic maybe." She held out a piece of paper for Hamed to take. He grimaced at finding that it was the bill. "I'll be sending out the fees for the other incidentals." Her arms gestured to her haggard and beaten entourage. With a polite but stiff farewell, she walked back to her group. They took a while longer to gather up themselves and their belongings before leaving Hamed and Onsi on the empty platform where Tram 015 sat deceptively still.

Hamed sighed wearily, looking down at the bill and trying not to think of the added costs to come. In truth, his mind was more consumed by what the sheikha had just revealed. All this time they'd been chasing the wrong lead. A Marid djinn wouldn't have helped, not with some foreign, unknown spirit. All that effort, wasted. The worst of it was, he had no idea what to do next. He was a seasoned investigator without a clue to go on. That was a depressing circumstance. Onsi, who stood beside him, was muttering beneath his breath.

"Do you have something to say, Agent Onsi?" Hamed asked testily.

"Oh, I was just thinking that it wasn't Turkic," he spoke up.

"What?" Hamed asked.

"Sheikha Nadiyaa suggested that the spirit was speaking a Turkic dialect," he explained. "But I don't think so. Yes, the stress falls on the last syllable just the same, but it didn't carry the same vowel harmony. Also, Turkic doesn't have any diphthongs...."

Hamed let him go on, sorry now that he had even asked.

"If I had to venture a guess," the man continued, pensively tapping his spectacles, "I'd say the spirit was speaking some form of archaic or classical Armenian."

Hamed's head shot up, and he rounded on Onsi, who stepped back under his glare. The shorter man yelped as Hamed went searching in his coat pockets, rifling about until he found what he sought—drawing it out. He held up the piece of sweet sudjukh between a thumb and forefinger before Onsi's nose, so that the man had to look at it cross-eyed. Then, in triumph, he growled out one word.

"Armenian!"

~

It turned out that Superintendent Bashir had the fortitude not of a devious mastermind, but a jellyfish. Once Hamed had confronted him with the evidence of his involvement with the foreign spirit, he had confessed everything in a torrent. That had been nearly twenty minutes ago. Now Bashir was collapsed completely onto his desk in the most undignified manner, wailing and slapping at his cheeks. He might have begun to pull out his hair, if he had much left to grasp. Hamed was all for contrition, but this had become ridiculous.

"That's enough," he snapped.

The superintendent choked back several sobs like a scolded child, reduced now to making a whimpering noise through his nostrils.

"Let me see if I understand this fully," Hamed began, going over the story he'd been told between the cries of self-pity. "You've been running a smuggling ring using Tram 015, shipping candies and pastries coming in from Armenia to the Old City."

It was an ingenious enterprise, when you considered it on the merits. The superintendent hadn't been the only one who'd taken a liking to sweet sudjukh. So had his wife, and his family. Her brother, it turned out, had contacts within the Armenian district in both Cairo and the Old City. What had begun as a few gifts from home, given as tokens in exchange for favors, had fast turned into a full-scale operation bringing in sudjukh by the barrel. They'd managed to corner the Armenian sweets market in scattered communities between here and Luxor. Everyone was getting a cut: the dirigibles from Alexandria shipping it in, the customs officers who ignored the tariffs, and, of course, Superintendent Bashir, who provided a steady and reliable means of transport for the goods.

"Only something went wrong with one of the shipments," Hamed continued. "And some Armenian spirit got smuggled in with one of your cargo. Do you know the penalty, superintendent, for transporting unregistered supernatural entities across Egypt's borders?"

Bashir took a deep swallow, shaking his head emphatically. "I would never involve myself in such a thing! As God is my witness, I took no offers for such contraband! And I would have forbidden attempts to do so! You must believe me!"

Hamed eyed the man appraisingly. Trafficking of mystical creatures into the country was a well-known problem to the Ministry. But smugglers usually traded in things like unhatched rukh eggs or re'em calves—selling unwary collectors infant animals that quickly grew into unmanageable monsters. There'd been a craze over lightning birds two years back. Just five of the things had wreaked havoc for days: disabling trams, shutting down factory machines, and setting off blackouts in the posher streets of Cairo now lined by electric lamps. The Ministry had to fly in a troupe of Sangoma diviners from Bambata City to recapture them. But Hamed had to admit that he couldn't believe anyone would have willingly smuggled in the ghastly spirit that now resided in Tram 015. More likely, the thing had snuck into a shipment while still in Armenia.

"When did you realize that you'd possibly contaminated your tram?" he asked Bashir.

The superintendent winced. "When I encountered it for myself. I heard it speak and knew right away it was Armenian. I sought to expel it from the tram. But when I told the Armenians about it. . . ."

"They became scarce," Hamed finished.

"They cut me out of my own trade!" Bashir cried, recapturing some of his indignation. "They claimed I was cursed and would have no more to do with me!" He shuddered. "Am I? Cursed, I mean?"

Hamed wished he could tell the man he was. "You're not cursed. But you have broken more laws than I can count!" He waved off Onsi, who seemed set to tick each one off. "You tried to keep the matter quiet, almost firing a worker who found out about the spirit. Then you kept the contaminated vehicle in service, so that nothing would look as if it were wrong. Only after the spirit attacked a passenger did you have the moral sense to ground the tram."

"It almost tore the woman to pieces!" Bashir exclaimed, waving his arms. "All I could think was what would have happened if the passenger had been harmed!

I couldn't have such a blight on my record! Or my conscience," he added hastily. "I put Tram 015 out of commission until I could find a way to fix things."

"That was when you lured us here under false pretenses," Hamed continued. "Even when you knew all along the source of the problem! If you'd been up front from the beginning, we wouldn't have wasted all this time. And several innocent women wouldn't have nearly been killed today!"

"I'm very disappointed by your unscrupulousness, Superintendent Bashir," Onsi said, shaking his head.

Bashir had the decency to hang his head, stung by the reprimand. A nice touch, Hamed thought. He sat back in his chair, tenting his fingers. "The question is, what do we do now?" Onsi mimicked Hamed's posture, though he needed to work on pulling it off. Perhaps a flourish first with his spectacles.

"What will you do?" the superintendent quavered.

Hamed shrugged nonchalantly. "We could become heroes. The men who broke up a smuggling ring and corruption in the transit sector. Oh, the dailies would love that headline!" Bashir's skin turned a lighter shade of beige, and he looked like he might faint. Hamed let the threat hang there for a while, letting the man's imagination work.

"But luckily for you we don't handle petty bureaucratic malfeasance." he said at last, sitting up and leaning forward. He ignored Onsi, who in trying a similar maneuver had almost fallen from his chair. "We're agents with the Ministry of Alchemy, Enchantments, and Supernatural Entities, and we're going to do as we set out to do—and solve the case of Tram 015!"

"You're not going to turn me in?" Bashir piped up, his voice reedy.

"No," Hamed answered magnanimously. It was just a *candy* smuggling ring, after all. A bit ridiculous when you thought about it.

The superintendent, however, was effusive with his praise. "Oh! God bless your head! Your eyes! God the Merciful look after you!"

Hamed let it go on for a while before holding up a hand to stop. That would do.

"You are, however, going to do no more smuggling or any other thing of the sort," he commanded. "From this day on you walk a straight path, Superintendent Bashir."

"Yes! Yes!" The man nodded in clear relief. "A straight path!"

Hamed stood, and Onsi with him. Pulling out a sheet of paper from his jacket, Hamed unfolded it and placed it face down on the desk before sliding it forward. Bashir picked it up, turning it over and reading in confusion.

"I don't understand, what's this?" he asked.

"The bill from Sheikha Nadiyaa," Hamed answered curtly. "You'll be getting a few more. Including one for repairs on a boilerplate eunuch, if I had to guess." Seeing the man's eyes glaze over as he did the calculations in his head, Hamed smiled. Picking up the bronze dish, he offered it up with a rattle of its contents. "More sweet sudjukh, Superintendent Bashir?"

CHAPTER FIVE

The post-work crowd had filled up Makka by early evening. And the chatter of their talk created a steady din of competing voices in the small space of the Nubian eatery. A group of factory women, in light blue dresses and gloves, debated heatedly with some iron workers—still donning soot-smeared aprons. Elsewhere, several constables in khakis shared tea with a turbaned vendor of used boiler-plate eunuch parts. The policemen laughed heartily as the man complained of his wife and daughters, who had gone to protest each day leaving him without his supper. Every tongue wagged about the impending vote for women's suffrage that was slated to take place tomorrow. The anticipation in the air was palpable, and it was hard for most Cairenes to not be swept up.

Hamed, however, eschewed talk of government affairs or social policy. He tiredly drank down a third cup of coffee and picked up another of the fragrant Abyssinian blend. Ethiopian brews had been steadily replacing the more common Turkish varieties in the city. The Amharic phrase *buna tetu,* literally "drink coffee," had even made its way into the polyglot that was Cairo's ever-expanding lexicon. Holding up the small blue porcelain cup, he sat staring into the face of the white foam topping and went over his long day.

The satisfaction he'd gotten at seeing Superintendent Bashir cowed (and it had been *immensely* satisfying) was short-lived. After leaving Ramses Station, they'd gone to the Ministry's library. The repository housed an extensive selection of volumes on supernatural entities, and they hoped to discover something of the unknown spirit haunting Tram Car 015. Their research had taken up the entire rest of the day, stretching into late afternoon. And yet, they'd found not the barest hint or scrap. All they had to show for their painstaking work was exhaustion.

He looked across the table to where Onsi sat relating the events of the past ten hours to their server—the very same young woman who had acquainted them with Sheikha Nadiyaa. Her name was Abla, they'd learned. She sat in a chair between them, eyes growing wider as she learned each detail. Hamed thought dimly to scold the man for discussing Ministry business with a civilian. But he was too tired at the moment to care. Besides, there was something about Abla that made you want to talk, almost like the words were being pulled off your tongue. He glanced with interest to her earrings—no longer the sacred cow of Hathor, but matching figurines of silver lionesses.

"Wait," she interrupted. "Slow down. Who's this Zagros?"

"The djinn who oversees the library at the Ministry," Onsi explained.

"I think I know a Zagros who works in Imbaba," she mused. "A small three-horned djinn? Designs milking machines for camels?"

Hamed downed his coffee, shaking his head. The way djinn all shared names, the last census probably had a page of Zagroses—even if it was a mountain range in Persia. "Another one," he said. "An elder Marid of some girth, with lavender scales, hair growing out of his nose and ears, and silver-capped tusks. Very particular about manuscripts."

The Ministry's librarian had directed them to resources that might help track down the spirit. About half a dozen versions of the tenth-century cosmography *Marvels of Things Created and Miraculous Aspects of Things Existing* by al-Qazwini. Endless medieval bestiaries detailing everything from basilisks to sea monsters supposedly as big as small islands. They'd even gone through a treatise on natural history by Pliny the Elder. The fussy djinn had stood watching over them the whole while, voicing disapproval with the way they handled the manuscripts and at times insisting on being the one to turn the delicate pages. The only thing that kept him placated was Onsi's unrestrained glee at perusing the archaic tomes—of which Zagros quite approved.

"Now that's a story," Abla said when the tale was done. She wore a hijab today in the red, green, and gold of the Egyptian Feminist Sisterhood, the words *Votes for Women* scripted throughout. "You Spooky Boys sure keep things lively. What's the plan now?"

"All we have to go on is that the spirit speaks Armenian," Hamed groused. "The library is fairly short on Armenian folklore. We'll probably go into an Armenian district tomorrow. Or visit one of the churches. See if anyone knows anything about spirits from their homeland."

Abla made a face. "I don't want to be rude, but people don't really like talking to you guys." Seeing their expressions, she shrugged. "Just being honest. Not your fault. I think it's because you're involved in matters that most people find unsettling. It's one thing to accept that djinn and magic are part of the world now. It's something else entirely to be so intimately tied to it. You weird folks out."

Hamed was near indignant. "You don't seem to have a problem talking to us," he countered.

Abla's eyes lowered to slits and she grinned. "Do I look like most people to you, Agent Hamed?" She stopped to tap her chin wistfully. "I think, though, I know someone who might talk to you. But you'll have to promise to buy me a doll. Or two."

Hamed stared at her puzzled, but listened.

~

"As you can well see, no two are alike," the older woman told them proudly. "I make each one with these very hands." She held up fingers that were wrinkled with age, but which held steady. "And name them as if they were my very own children."

Hamed looked up from where he sat on a mahogany divan upholstered in yellow and decorated with emerald green pillows. Wooden shelves arranged in rows of three lined the tiled mosaic walls of the small square room that held the faint scent of recently burned incense. Dolls sat on all of them, their sculpted faces glistening beneath the light of alchemical lamps and smiling down from behind wide-open eyes and thick black lashes. Each one was indeed different, in hair and hue and features—a slight fullness to the lips here, a curly mane there. Their dress was just as varied, displaying the garb of diverse nations and peoples.

In truth, Hamed was a bit discomfited by them. There was something slightly off about dolls. Too close to real people, without ever quite achieving it. And children at that, with freakishly small hands and infantile faces trapped in place. Perhaps he'd drunk too much coffee, but he kept imagining them coming alive with jerking movements and jumping down to grab at him with those tiny hands.

Trying to ignore the things, he turned his attention back to the woman in the chair opposite them. Putting on a smile, he said, "You do exquisite work, Madaam Mariam. It is to be highly commended." He lifted his tea and cleared his throat as he sipped.

"Oh yes!" Onsi, who shared the divan with him, said at once. "Wonderful work! My sisters all had dolls when younger, and I have never seen any that look so lifelike."

Too lifelike, Hamed thought silently, but kept up his smile.

They had found Madaam Mariam's shop just where Abla had said they would: an unassuming store at the night market of Khan-el Khalili, marked by a set of deep red doors. The doll maker had been fast at work at their arrival, seated at a table where she was constructing her latest creation. It lay unfinished now, the reflective eyes meant to fit into its smiling face sitting out like forgotten marbles amid the various tools of her trade.

The doll maker accepted their compliments, blushing beneath her olive complexion. She sipped at her small rose-colored cup of tea while drawing a green silk shawl more securely over her shoulders. Otherwise she was dressed plainly, in a long brown workman's apron over a white kaftan embroidered with blue flowers.

"You young men today are so free with your compliments," she chortled. "I was never one of the very pretty ones that was looked at for so long. Now my sister, oh what a beauty! Long dark hair, such exquisite cheeks—like my dolls. Men lost their heads around her!" Her eyes creased around the edges at the memory. "But me? I learned that when men spent time giving me compliments, they were usually after something. Even when they gave me small presents, like a bag of sweet sudjukh." She inclined her head to Onsi in gratitude. It had been his idea, after all. "So then, agents, why is it the two of you have come to spend your night sipping tea with an old doll maker and give compliments so freely?"

Hamed set his cup down on a tray next to a long-spouted brass Turkish teapot, choosing his next words carefully. "We were referred to you by Abla." At the doll maker's blank stare, he amended his words. "I mean, Siti." It was some kind of nickname, he supposed, but the woman had told them to use it.

Madaam Mariam's face lit up. "Ah, Siti! Do you know that I have known her since she was a girl? Her mother had a tailoring shop right here next to mine then, and I would sometimes look after her. I made her first dolls. She still stops in to buy one, from time to time."

Hamed nodded. It had been odd to find out that, of all things, Abla collected dolls. Supposedly she had dozens. "She told us you were a great doll maker," he went on. "She also said that you were a storyteller, and often shared tales from Armenia."

Madaam Mariam laughed deep and rich. "Do not tell me the Ministry has sent you all this way to hear my silly stories! Wouldn't you rather buy a doll instead? Maybe as a gift to a daughter or a niece?" She leaned in to whisper. "Siti would certainly like one, if you're thinking of courting her."

It was Hamed's turn to blush. "Agent Onsi and I will both certainly buy one of your wonderful dolls, each, before leaving. But we'd also love to hear your stories. In fact, we have one to tell you, if you'll listen?"

She gave him a brooding look but accepted. Hamed exchanged glances with Onsi, and over the course of the next few minutes, they took turns talking about the spirit haunting Tram 015. When they finished, both men sat back and waited.

Madaam Mariam remained quiet for a while. She turned to stare at a painting above her work desk, one of the few spaces not taken up with dolls. It depicted Saint George in Byzantine style, slaying a great twisting serpent. Beside it sat a small slab of reddish stone carved with a cross, with the horizontal tricolor flag of Armenian independence hanging beneath. Her gaze seemed inward, though, going through some mental inventory. Every few moments she touched at the ornate striped scarf that held back her single gray braid. When she did speak, her voice was hushed.

"An al!" she whispered. "That is what you describe. It can be no other."

Hamed played the word over in his head, eagerness mingling with unfamiliarity. "An al? I've never heard of any such spirit."

"Why would you?" Madaam Mariam asked. "There should not be an al in Cairo. The alk, as their kind are known, are said to live in the waters and mountains back in Armenia, in far off places where most do not go." She stopped in thought. "Though I have heard Persians, Tajiks, and others claim alk can be found in their lands—by different names. I have never seen an al myself, but my grandmother used to tell me stories. She would speak of alk that looked like ugly old crones, with sharp fangs, long wild hair, great long copper claws and teeth, with breasts that sagged to their knees!"

Hamed listened intently. The spirit in the tram was not so fantastic, but there were enough similarities. "What would an al want?" he asked.

The doll maker wrinkled her face in thought "My grandmother told stories of alk who stole people's livers or tempted men to marry only to later devour them. But in most of her tales, an al would go after women—to steal their babies."

Hamed frowned. "Why would the spirit want a baby?"

Madaam Mariam shrugged. "The stories sometimes claimed they ate babies. Or the al would take the baby to raise as its own. It was never any one thing. But they were forever after babies. Sometimes they'd trick women into giving up their babes, then rip out their tongues when they tried to cry out! Others might creep into your house at night, steal the baby, and leave you with a monster that took your baby's face. A few stories even said an al would snatch the unborn baby right out of a woman's belly, then eat her entrails after."

The doll maker shuddered at this last part and stopped to pour herself more tea.

"You're saying the spirit that attacked us wanted a baby?" Hamed asked.

"Pardon my interruption, Agent Hamed," Onsi interjected. "But the spirit didn't attack all of us. Oh, it pushed us from the tram car that first time, but that was all. This morning when it attacked, it didn't come after me. I don't think it came after you either."

Hamed thought back on the chaotic scene. Onsi was

right. The spirit hadn't attacked him. It had knocked him aside only after he got in its way. "It went after the women!" he exclaimed.

Onsi nodded. "And the only passenger it attacked was a woman as well. I believe I understand now why it tore at the women's clothing. It wasn't trying to kill them, at least not right away."

Hamed recalled the spirit slashing furiously away at the women, not to injure but to rip apart their clothing—all around the belly. "It was searching for a woman with child," he finished. Struck by the realization, he turned back to the doll maker. "How do we stop it?"

Madaam Mariam sipped her tea before answering. "You will need iron, to bind it. Something sharp, preferably. Even as small as a needle. Prick the spirit. Then, once that is done, bring it home and make it work for you."

Hamed squinted back at her. "That's a bit strange."

"Most of these stories are," she told him flatly. "Now, that is all I can tell you about the al and I wish the both of you good fortune." She smiled, waving a hand across her showroom. "In the meanwhile, may I interest you in a doll?"

"A baby-eating Armenian spirit is haunting a Cairo tram," Abla repeated. "Well, I have to admit, I didn't see that coming." They sat once more in the restaurant. The evening crowd had thinned out. Except for two men playing a board game, only the three of them were left. Hamed and Onsi shared a late meal of boiled potatoes in a flavorful stew and chicken cooked in a spicy red chili sauce, which Abla had graciously set aside for them. She had pulled up a chair, admiring the two dolls that lay packaged inside decorated green painted boxes.

"Not just Armenian," Onsi answered, tearing up bits of a flatbread to dip into the stew. "It seems these alk are known all through Central Asia and the Caucuses."

It turned out Madaam Mariam had been right about that after all. They'd returned to the Ministry's library with a name, and this time Zagros had helped them mine a wealth of information. There still wasn't anything on Armenia specifically, but some variation of the spirit appeared in numerous texts. They were often part of the local folklore in remote and isolated places little touched by the modern world. In rural Persia, they were known as āl; among herding communities of Tajiks and Pashtuns, ol, hāl, yāl; and in villages that lined the forgotten trade routes of the Caucuses, as everything from almasti to the al-karis.

In a few instances, the spirits were described as

male—said to be old men with flowing hair who lived in deep rivers, emerging at night to make mischief for farmers. But in the main, the al was a woman. Sometimes she was a beautiful young woman who lived in bushes and streams or dark mountain passages, allowing men only glimpses of her. In other stories, she was an old and monstrous crone—a hag with sharp rending claws. Across the many different peoples and nations, the one constant of these female al was that they stalked women with child, either that or the child itself—both newly born or still in the womb. Some stole the infants, drank the blood of pregnant women, or even removed the vital organs of mothers to prevent them from nursing.

"It's all very gruesome business," Onsi concluded, after Hamed had related much of this.

Abla huffed. "It all sounds like something you men would dream up."

Hamed frowned. "We didn't make this up. The spirit is real enough. In fact, it seems these kinds of harmful spirits dealing with childbirth are known the world over and are almost invariably female in nature. The Churel of India, La Llorona of the Americas, the Lamia of old Greece . . ." There were so many he and Onsi had to make up their minds not to research every last one, or they'd have been there all night. Some Persian folklore even claimed the al was a distant relative to the djinn, though

Zagros had puffed up so furiously at the suggestion Hamed had let the matter drop.

"Female in nature," Abla repeated, unfazed by the litany. "And what does that mean to a spirit? You said it yourself, it was just some gray smoke before it took form. There are whole theories that claim spirit beings have no shape in our realm and take after the forms we give them in our stories."

Onsi inhaled in excitement. "You've been reading some of the recent Coptic philosophers' applications of Thomas Aquinas's studies of being to al-Jahiz's writings on the djinn!" he exclaimed.

Abla merely wriggled her fingers. "I've dabbled. Here's what I think. That spirit was just a formless being minding its own business. Then, it encountered men. And they decided to make it this beautiful woman or this monstrous crone, because that's the only way many men can even view women. Maybe they were looking for a way to explain why their wives died in childbirth, or why infants died in their blankets. Maybe they were just afraid of old women. So, they made up this al, conjured it up as a woman, and blamed it on her!"

Hamed's head was spinning. That people—men, at that—were responsible for some child-stealing spirit boggled the mind. But Abla appeared thoroughly convinced by her reasoning.

"A fascinating theory!" Onsi commended.

"Except," Hamed put in, "if what you say is possible, women could have thought up the al just as easily."

Abla shook her head sternly. "No woman would ever think up something so ridiculous."

Hamed gave up. This was not an argument he was going to win. "Well, however the al that is haunting Tram Car 015 came about," he said, changing topics, "we still need to find a way to get it out of there."

Their research had come across quite a few ways, each one more inventive than the last. There were the usual preventives: incense burning and amulets. Remnants of the old religions prescribed charms and spells. Both Muslims and Christians had particular verses to protect pregnant women and newborns in regions where alk were feared. More extreme cases called for hanging the entrails of animals outside the home, to confuse the spirit into taking that bloody offering instead. Getting rid of an al was harder work.

In parts of the Persian countryside, farmers claimed a man had to grab an al by the nose and hold it until it returned the stolen baby—and the mother's organs. Tajiks maintained that certain pungent herbs found in their homeland, when properly burned, chased away an al. Some Pashtuns held that the trick was fire—and that flames would drive an al fleeing from homes and holy places. None of those was particularly appealing, especially the idea of grabbing that thing's nose or setting the tram on fire. There was one remedy, however, that they encountered repeatedly.

"Iron," Hamed stated, after he'd gone through the list. "In many stories, iron is used to exorcize an al."

"In Khorasan, villagers place iron objects under the pillow or bed of pregnant women," Onsi related. "And they might tie a small bit of iron, like a needle, around a baby's neck."

"Some Pashtun tales claim a man must threaten an al with an iron shovel to drive it off," Hamed added. "Stories throughout the Caucuses instruct people in remote regions to place a knife, scissor, farming tool—anything iron—at the top of doors or the bottom of chimneys to keep an al out."

"Auntie Mariam told you iron was used to dispel alk in Armenia," Abla said, catching on.

"Precisely," Hamed said. "We figure since this spirit seems to come from Armenia, best to use an Armenian practice."

"Makes sense," she nodded approvingly, before her eyes lit up. "Wait here!"

Jumping up from her chair she disappeared into a back room, almost running in her brown boots. She returned shortly, grinning wide and holding a small black object in her right hand. A dagger, Hamed realized in surprise.

"Something iron," she said. With a dazzling flourish, she twirled the blade nimbly between her fingers and offered it to Hamed hilt first. His eyebrows climbed at the display, and not for the first time he wondered exactly who Abla—or, perhaps, Siti—truly was.

"You have my thanks," he said, accepting the dagger. "Though the way you spoke before, I thought you might not want us to exorcize the spirit."

Her grin vanished, replaced with a fierce look that made her dark eyes glitter. "It eats babies," she all but growled. "Cute, fat, innocent little babies. Who does that? To hell with that monster. Put it down!"

Hamed dipped his head solemnly, feeling as if he were accepting a command and not a request. "We still have one problem," he said as she sat again. "The spirit is on to us, we think. It only showed itself to Sheikha Nadiyaa because it knew there were women about. The previous attack it carried out was also on a woman. It chases men off, but it won't take form for us. What would be ideal is a pregnant woman to draw it out."

"I hope the two of you have realized that no woman with child would be fool enough to be used as bait for a murderous spirit," Abla replied. "She'd probably send all her brothers and relatives after you for even suggesting it."

"We have," Hamed assured her. "And we'd never do such a thing." Onsi and he had discussed the matter on the way back to the restaurant. They'd agreed not to put any more civilians knowingly in harm's way. There were women agents at the Ministry—but those were very few in number. The only one in Cairo, as far as he knew, didn't even wear dresses. Besides, this was their case, he thought firmly. It was up to them to see it through.

"I've been thinking on that problem," Onsi said, wiping his fingers from some powdered pastries. "I think there may be a way to draw out the spirit by tricking it." He paused, his round face going a bit hesitant. "Do you remember I told you that back at Oxford, I was in the Dramatic Society and played Katherina in *The Taming of the Shrew*? Well, it was generally agreed that I was quite good."

As Onsi put forth his plan, Hamed groaned. Abla, on the other hand, could barely contain her squeals of delight.

CHAPTER SIX

That next morning, Ramses Station was abuzz with activity. People had been pouring into the transportation hub since dawn, coming in by tram from throughout Cairo and on airships from all over the country. They were overwhelmingly women: young and old, Copts and Muslims, in trendy urban styles or the more traditional dress, in factory-worker smocks and nurse's uniforms, in school outfits and professional government attire. They came with placards and banners naming their towns and villages and cities, chanting, clapping and singing as they joined the swelling crowds. Signs calling for the vote were everywhere, many with images of activists and even a few with the queen. A sprawling flag bearing the Janus-faced Hatshepsut symbol of the Egyptian Feminist Sisterhood hung from an upper railing beside another bearing the words THE WOMEN OF '79 LIVE ON! The atmosphere was nothing less than electric as everyone waited at this historic spot to hear parliament's decision on granting the greatest right to the majority of Egypt's populace.

Hamed fidgeted with the veil covering his face as he

and Onsi walked across the floor of Ramses Station. When he had agreed to the younger man's plan, he had hoped that they would simply don gallabiyahs, still worn in public by men and women in more rural areas. But Abla had insisted that wouldn't do and managed to find an all-night tailor in the Khan who could have something done in hours. The man had been as good as his word, fitting and preparing dresses for them to pick up by morning. For such short notice, the garments were decidedly fancy—all white and fashioned in the mix of Parisian and Egyptian styles popular among upper-class Cairene women, with matching round hats covered in semi-sheer veils that wrapped their faces in small clouds.

Despite his discomfort, Hamed had to admit Onsi's logic had been sound. The spirit would only appear to women. So if they were going to draw it out themselves, they needed to be seen as women. It was commonly known that spirits had a peculiar tunnel-vision when it came to such things. Dress an inanimate object as a person, and they took it for just that. Leave out some rocks instead of food, and they'd try to devour them. For many spirits, perception was reality. Thus, it only stood to reason that this al would take them for what it sought, if they looked the part.

That was easier said than done.

For about the third time, Hamed nearly stumbled in

the short white heels that matched his long dress. How modern women got about in these things he couldn't possibly figure out. What made it worse were the extra pounds he carried—a great deal of stuffing that made his stomach bulge out to mimic a woman with child. Onsi had sought to make them play their parts perfectly, going as far as to weigh down the cushioned prosthesis with dense material. It made for a heavy load to bear.

"You have to keep your feet spread apart!" Onsi instructed, sidling up to him. He spoke loudly to be heard above the noisy crowds. "Imagine that you're a penguin and do like so." His legs took on a waddling quality and he seemed to move with ease, his stuffed belly protruding before him.

It was probably easier when you had nine sisters, Hamed grumbled silently. But he mimicked the walk and it did indeed make it somewhat more bearable. By the time they'd made it to the lift he had already grown weary. The trip up to the aerial tram yard allowed him a brief rest before the doors opened to Cairo's morning skyline and they made their way to their destination.

Tram 015 sat quiet and isolated on the platform. There was something ominous about its stillness—as if the car was waiting for them. "Are you ready?" Hamed asked, tamping down his unease.

"Ready," Onsi replied, a slight quaver to his voice.

Hamed looked to the younger man and saw the eyes behind his silver spectacles somewhat wide. He remembered then how nervous he'd been as a recruit, confronting a truly dangerous situation for the first time.

"I always keep in mind that I'm a Ministry agent," he offered in encouragement. "Whatever we're facing might be older, stronger, and have powers beyond us. But that's what we were trained for, and nothing is invincible. Also, a few prayers help."

Onsi nodded appreciatively. "I've done quite a bit of praying. I think I'll be fine."

"Then let's get this over with. Remember, we only need to prick it." Hiking up his dress, Hamed walked forward to the door of Tram 015 and pulled it open.

The inside of the car looked much like they'd last left it. No one had come in to clean, with the Transportation Union citing safety concerns. Dried flecks of blood from the hapless chickens streaked some of the windows, and a smear containing white feathers ran along the floor. Bits and pieces of food left over from the altar lay scattered about as well, alongside the wooden tray, stool, and cages that had been reduced to splintered sticks.

Hamed picked his way through the debris and took a seat at one end of the car, grasping a pole to lower himself down. It felt good to sit. The cushions beside him showed deep furrows where the spirit had slashed through during their last encounter. He kept his vision forward and tried not to think about the claws that had done such damage. From the corners of his eyes, however, he searched above. He found the ethereal gray smoke right away, lazily weaving its way through the clockwork mechanics of the tram, its movements illuminated by each flicker of the ceiling lamp. He cast a glance to the other end of the car, where Onsi had seated himself in turn. They were in place. Sitting back, he waited. It wasn't too long before they heard the locking mechanisms holding the tram in place begin to tumble.

They had arranged this with Bashir. He and Onsi had agreed that to pull off this ruse, Tram 015 had to be up and running again—to make them look like ordinary passengers. Bashir had reluctantly agreed to put the car on an old unused line that ran a quick circuit through the center of Cairo. Somewhere along the way, they hoped the al would take the bait and reveal itself.

There was an audible hiss of steam as the mooring clamps released, and the tram joggled in its descent from the aerial yards to the main docks below. Hamed watched through the curtained windows as they passed down between a webbing of steel girders. He risked a peek at the gray smoke. It had begun to move faster in seeming anticipation. A good sign. Glancing down the other end of the car he found Onsi sitting peaceably. The man had retrieved two long iron needles from a bag and taken to knitting. He hummed a lullaby as he worked, stopping once in a while to rub his cushioned belly affectionately. Hamed managed to pull his eyes away from the spectacle and felt with reassurance for the black dagger nestled in a pocket sewn into his dress. The weapon was surprisingly light, weighted for Abla, he assumed—a puzzle he still couldn't quite fit together. A slight jolt pulled his attention back to the window. They had reached the latticework of corded cables that snaked across Cairo's skyway. Above came the sound of the pulley systems latching onto the proper line—and Tram 015 began to move.

The car streaked out over the city with a lurch. Its engines hummed and rattled as it went, accompanied by the familiar squeal of the pulley that moved along the cable. Every few seconds bright blue flashes lit up the interior, as outside electric bolts were thrown up with a piercing crackle. The ride was smooth, with a gentle swaying motion that easily lulled passengers to sleep. No chance of that today. It was all Hamed could do to not tap his feet anxiously as he waited for something to happen. He passed the time staring through the window, watching other trams zip by on their lines, turning this way and that as they transported Cairo's masses.

When the al did appear beside him, he almost jumped.

Hamed wasn't certain when the spirit had moved or taken shape. One moment the thing had been smoke, making its rounds in the gears above. The next it was here—taking the familiar form of a girl with moon-pale skin touched by gray. She sat on a seat next to him wearing that simple bone-white dress and looking fragile as a statue crafted of eggshell. Her delicate features were almost childlike beneath the flowing silver tresses that reached to her waist. And she stared up at him with generous pitch-black eyes that seemed to ripple.

Drawing a breath, Hamed turned slowly toward the al. A thin set of blue-tinged lips parted in a smile, revealing small teeth that glistened like pearls. She croaked out something in that grating voice he couldn't understand, tilting her head curiously. When he didn't answer, she pointed to his round belly with a slender finger and began making soft, cooing sounds. Wrapping her arms into a cradle, she rocked them back and forth and trilled something that sounded like "nani bala" repeatedly in a singsong.

When she finally reached a hand out to touch his stomach he flinched, remembering all too well the stories that said these kinds of diversions always preceded an al attack. She laughed richly at his flightiness, and he couldn't help but think of a predator toying with its prey. Of course, he was a diversion as well.

Just above the spirit's head, Hamed watched as Onsi came closer. He had gotten up as soon as the al settled down, and now stalked forward, a knitting needle gripped in his hand. He hummed his lullaby as he came and Hamed only wished he would move faster. The spirit continued her chatter unawares, too busy taking delight in her taunting ritual to register his movement. Onsi was so close now that Hamed could see the light glinting off the iron end of the needle. Lifting the makeshift weapon, Onsi stopped, poised to strike. There was a brief lull and inside Hamed a warning siren went off.

In stopping to ready his blow, Onsi had also ended his lullaby. The gut of silence in the emptied tram was louder than sound itself, and the al stopped short. She frowned as she caught the direction of Hamed's gaze, and looked up to see Onsi almost upon her.

Everything that happened next went by so fast Hamed could barely keep track. The girl let out a hiss upon seeing Onsi. In a blur she was gone, replaced with the hag. Standing to her full height, she swatted at Onsi with her claws, sending him tumbling away without even the opportunity to deliver the blow. Hamed acted on instinct, pulling out his dagger and lunging. He was surprised when he fell flat in the aisle, the sharp point of the weapon striking the floor. He had missed! The al had moved unexpectedly fast, angling out the way before he could reach her.

Realizing that a trap had been set for her, the hag extended a mouth of jagged teeth impossibly wide to let out a fierce screech. But the two men had prepared for that as well, stuffing their ears with cotton. Her voice grated and their heads rang, but they weren't incapacitated. Scrambling back up to his feet, Hamed brandished the dagger at the spirit. On the other end of the tram, Onsi too now stood, a knitting needle in each hand.

"Close the gap!" Hamed yelled, walking forward. Onsi nodded vigorously, doing the same.

The al twisted her head about, glaring at each man from behind the empty pits on her shriveled face. She screeched in threat, slashing out with her claws, but didn't press an attack. Her eyeless gaze warily regarded the iron they held, and she shrank away in what Hamed hoped was genuine fear. Still, this wouldn't be easy. A well-placed rake could eviscerate them if they weren't careful, and more than once he had to jump back before regaining the momentum. It was during this laborious advance that the spirit did something unanticipated. Lifting her claws above her head, she plunged them into the gears covering the ceiling. They didn't tear through the clockwork brain, but instead sank into the machinery like smoke. A sudden tremor ran through the tram and it zoomed forward with a terrific burst.

Hamed went flying back, swept off his feet, the dagger pitching from his hand. He landed hard on his side and was forced to clutch at a pole as the car continued to pick up speed. He cursed aloud. They should have foreseen that the spirit, after having spent so much time in the tram, would have found a way to control it! He looked up to find Onsi tumbling along the other end, trying desperately to catch hold of something. The al threw back her head to cackle wildly at their distress. Hamed was wondering how this could possibly get worse—when it did.

A sudden swerve sent him rolling. When he managed to right himself he looked out the windows at the front of the tram to see they were going in another direction. The spirit had caused the car to switch cables! They were no longer on the old unused circuit, but on the city's main lines! His worst fears were realized as he caught sight of another tram fast approaching them, its horns blaring in alarm at what would be a certain collision.

Hamed held his breath, overcome with a sinking feeling of helplessness, when at the last moment, their tram switched sharply to another line. The other tram passed by at an angle, moving away at rapid speed. But Hamed could still see the faces of its terrified passengers, no doubt drenched in the same cold sweat as he was. On hearing the spirit cackle again, he found his fear turning to anger. Looking up, he searched along the walls until he found a dangling handle on a chain in the corner. With effort, he raised himself up along the pole, and began making his way to it.

He took barely controlled steps toward the pulley, holding onto the backs of bolted chairs or whatever he could to draw himself forward. The tram's speed didn't help, nor did its switching lines twice again. But he was determined to get there, spurred on by the infuriating laughter of the spirit. It was one thing to place their lives in danger. But now this monster thought it could come to his city and cause such mayhem! *That* he wasn't having! At last close enough, he extended a hand and tried for the pulley. He missed on the first attempt, and nearly fell back on the second—but on the third try he got his fingers firmly around it and pulled.

He held to the back of a seat as the car slowed to a grinding stop. There was the sound of engines dying then humming back to life. When the car moved again, it was in the opposite direction. The pulley was created for emergencies. It rerouted the tram to return home, making that its sole priority. With some fast turns, it switched lines, finding the unused circuit and heading back to Ramses Station. The al reacted in fury to this intervention, trying desperately to make the car go the way she wanted. But the tram refused, keeping to its predetermined course.

"It's done!" Hamed told her. He'd gotten hold of the dagger again and held it before him. On the other side, Onsi had recovered and stood waiting. "You might as well give over!"

The al glared at him, baring her jagged teeth in contempt. In a blur she disappeared, becoming smoke again and entering the clockwork gears. The grating sound of her voice thundered throughout the car and it shook violently. Hamed recognized it quickly, even in the unfamiliar language—a curse. She was cursing the tram. Sparks erupted from the gears as once again the car picked up speed. It raced along the cable, setting off a high-pitched squeal and endless blue bolts of electricity. As he saw Ramses Station appearing rapidly through the front windows, he realized with dread what the al was planning.

"Grab onto something!" he yelled to Onsi, as he did the same. "She's going to crash—!"

Hamed never finished his warning as the world turned violently upside down. He was spinning about, striking bolted down furniture as he tried to keep his limbs drawn in close. Nothing made sense, and he could barely tell what was happening. There was a terrific clamor of noise and a jarring sensation that made even his teeth shake—then finally came quiet and stillness.

Blinking, Hamed lifted his head to look about the tram, trying to figure out how the chairs had gotten onto the ceiling. It took a moment to make out that it wasn't the ceiling he was looking at, and that the chairs were where they'd always been. The car had reached the platform but had been wrenched off its pulley. It now appeared to be laying on its side and he was squeezed between two seats where he'd landed. Everything hurt, but as he checked, nothing appeared to be broken. He was gathering his voice to call out for Onsi when a set of long claws gripped the seats above him and a ghastly face emerged to peer down.

The hag grinned in triumph. Hamed tried to lift the dagger he'd managed somehow to hold onto, but couldn't bring it to bear at this angle. The al cackled and hissed, bending her shriveled head closer so that it was only inches from his own. Her breath, so cold it left flakes of ice on his moustache, held a fetid stink that filled his nostrils. He braced for an attack from those savage jaws, but abruptly the spirit lifted up, listening.

Hamed listened too. As his senses returned he could just make out a sound—a steady chanting that seemed to be building. The voices of women. Hundreds of women, gathered on the station floor. The al let out an eager cry and in a blur had become smoke again. It shot up through the smashed windows of the tram directly above and disappeared.

"Onsi!" Hamed cried out hoarsely. "Onsi! Are you alright?"

"Here!" the man groaned from nearby. "Roughed up, but I can manage. And you?"

"I'll be fine," he answered back, struggling to rise.

"The spirit!" Onsi called. "I fear it's gone—"

"I know." Hamed grit his teeth. They had succeeded in exorcising the al from Tram 015, only to send it into a sea of unsuspecting women below.

~

It seemed to take a painfully long time to extricate themselves from the overturned tram car as Hamed fretted. Then the ride down in the lift took interminable minutes more. He paced in place, counting down the floor numbers on the dial above. In his head, he scolded himself for not taking the stairs, though he knew that would have only taken longer. It was just his worry talking, but he had reason to be anxious. When the silver doors of the lift finally opened he bounded out, pushing past the boilerplate eunuch attendant and bracing for nothing less than blood and mayhem.

The floor of Ramses Station had grown more crowded, if that was possible. There were people everywhere—women, in the main, with some men who had joined them and a few djinn. They filled the hall and upper balconies, chanting and waving signs, some of them with slogans painted on their hands and cheeks. It was with relief that the horror he'd expected to find hadn't come to pass. He didn't doubt the al was here. It wouldn't be able to help itself, not with this many women around. But maybe it had decided subtlety was best.

"How will we ever find it in all of this?" Onsi lamented.

"We're investigators," Hamed told him, already scanning the vast crowds. "We're trained to see what other people would just pass by. Don't look at everything. There's too much. Instead, try to find what doesn't belong. What doesn't fit in."

"What doesn't belong," Onsi muttered. He repeated it like a mantra until exclaiming, "Oh! There!"

Hamed nodded, impressed with the younger man's acuity. He'd made out the spirit too, somewhere further in, close to the feet of the colossal statue of the pharaoh Ramses. It had taken the form of the girl, whose pale skin and bone-white slip assuredly looked out of place. She walked the floor of the hall barefoot, drinking in everything with her mouth parted in wonder. Women everywhere, as far as those hungry black eyes could see. She must have felt like a child let loose in a sweetshop, Hamed thought darkly. Reaching for the dagger in his dress, he started forward.

At least he tried to. Only their path was blocked by the sheer mass of people. They attempted to push through, but made little progress. He was wondering how'd they'd ever make their way when Onsi began shouting in a high voice.

"Can't you see there are women with child here?" he cried. "Have Cairenes lost all manners? What a scandal! Will no one let us pass?"

Hamed stared in open admiration. The man really threw himself into a role! He'd almost forgotten they were still in their garb—and veiled at that. The dramatic appeals worked. People parted for them, admonishing those who didn't move fast enough. Soon they had a clear path directly toward the al. But what he now saw made the pit of his stomach go hollow.

The al had chosen her prey: a woman who stood somewhat apart, watching the crowds and holding a swaddled baby in her arms. Stopping beside her, the spirit began her ritual, smiling and cooing at the infant. Looking down at the girl, the woman smiled, and bent slightly to show the face of her newborn. The al's eyes widened. Cradling her thin arms, she rocked them back and forth before the woman with a querying look. Hamed moved faster, shouting and struggling to be heard above the cacophony as his heart pounded in panic.

But his warning was unneeded.

Perhaps it was the strangeness of the pale silver-haired girl. Or just a mother's instinct. But the woman drew back and shook her head politely. She turned away and resumed looking at the crowd. Undaunted, the al reached out and tugged at her arm, still smiling inquisitively. The woman pulled away and this time retorted with words and a look that didn't appear at all polite. The spirit's smile vanished at that, storming over to anger. In a blur, she changed.

The hag that towered in the girl's place looked more frightening in the light that shined through the plain glass windows of Ramses Station than it had in the gloom of the tram. Her pale gray skin looked as if it had been stretched too taut over her elongated body, where ribs and clavicle showed beneath. Rounded bumps of bone lined her spine, leading to legs that bent back like the hindquarters of an animal. She swung an empty rotted gaze above the heads of the crowd, opening her jaws wide—and screeched.

The mother with her infant, who had watched the horror unfold mere feet away, screamed. So too did anyone else who happened to be near, many of them running and staggering away from the al. The spirit's wail had cut across the chanting in the hall, echoing even louder in the wide space and sending many to clutching their ears.

When they recovered to catch sight of the nightmare in their midst, the whole crowd, as if sharing one mind, began to back away.

Hamed and Onsi fought harder to move forward now, amid bodies desperately pushing in the opposite direction. But it was little use; they were dragged along like a tide. Near the al, only one person was left. Hamed saw to his horror that it was the mother and infant. The woman stood rooted to the spot, gripped by fear. Her arms clutched her infant protectively, eyes fixed on the looming danger. Having secured her prey, the hag turned back to the woman in triumph and all but salivated at the baby in her arms.

Hamed lifted his dagger. It was an impossible throw, but if he could just strike the spirit that might be enough. He stumbled to get his footing so he could brace himself properly and said a prayer to the most Merciful and Beneficent God to make his aim true.

But someone was suddenly in his way.

It was another woman, wearing a long black gallabiyah over her plump frame. She'd run up to stand behind the al and was shouting. The hag twisted its neck around and gave a short screeching burst in threat. But the woman stood her ground, holding up an object fastened to a necklace. It was a hamsa, Hamed recognized in surprise—a blue painted amulet shaped like the open palm of the right hand with an eye in the center. An old symbol, it was still popular in the countryside as a protective against evil. The woman was wielding it now like a weapon and calling out surahs at the top of her lungs.

The al turned fully now, lifting one of those massive clawed hands to cut down the bothersome interloper. But from out of the crowd, another woman appeared—this one in colorful Nubian prints. She held up an open palm, where a hamsa had been inscribed in henna, and added her own unwavering voice. Hamed watched in astonishment as more women ran forward, joining in chanting at the spirit and making warding gestures with their hands. One younger woman had gotten directly in front of the stricken mother, taking off her stylish Parisian hat covered in blue ostrich feathers and shaking it before the hag's face.

The spirit turned this way and that, hissing and raising her claws menacingly. But she seemed stunned by the show of these bold women, who had banded together to protect one of their own. And that was precisely what Hamed needed.

Many in the crowd had stopped to watch the odd happenings, and he had been able to push forward, finally breaking through to the front. Running up on his heeled shoes, he kept to the back of the bewildered and distracted spirit, staying out of her sight. When he pulled the dagger this time and struck at her exposed back, he didn't miss.

The al cried in pain or anger as the blade scored a length across the bones of her spine. Where the iron cut skin, acrid gray smoke rose up. She flung out a thick bony arm, sending Hamed sprawling back across the floor. He heard many in the crowd gasp, some coming to help him, thinking a pregnant woman had been hurt. With their aid, he sat up in time to see the al stalking forward, its hollow gaze seeming to recognize him, that horrid mouth of jagged teeth pulling back in a rictus. Catching his breath, he fought to speak, getting out one word.

"Stop!"

The hag went immediately still, poised in mid-step, one clawed hand raised high. Hamed felt a swelling relief as he watched the spirit stand quivering in place. Many of the stories said that once you pricked an al with iron, you could force her to do your bidding. He was overjoyed to see that part of the tale worked. Making it to his feet, he pushed away the hands trying to hold him back and walked up to the spirit. Coming to stand just beneath her tall frame, he stared up and perched on his toes to meet her straining face.

"Step back," he ordered crisply.

The al let loose a harried whine but began to walk backward. Her long limbs moved jerkily, making cracking noises as she went—but go she did. Hamed watched in satisfaction as the hag took up a pose like a statue, arms fixed at her sides even as her face shook in open contempt.

Onsi came running up then, huffing, his identification held up high as he addressed the shackled spirit: "Under the authority of the Ministry of Alchemy, Enchantments, and Supernatural Entities, we hereby take you into custody for breach of numerous regulations governing paranormal persons and sentient creatures, beginning with Article—!"

Hamed decided that this time he wouldn't mind listening to Onsi tick off each violation, but the younger man was interrupted by a girl running into the hall and shouting, her high voice breaking the quiet that had descended. What now, Hamed wondered? Several other people picked up the first cry, carrying and repeating what had been said. It was as the words reached him that the whole of Ramses Station erupted into a deafening cheer.

"The vote passed! We won! We won!"

Swept up in the jubilation, Hamed found he was cheering as well.

EPILOGUE

It was well into night as Agent Hamed sat typing up his report. The Ministry had emptied early as it always did on a Thursday before the Friday weekend. With the crowds still celebrating in the streets, most of the staff had left well before sunset. Granting suffrage to women had not been a universal sentiment. But now that it was done, hardly a person could be found who had before opposed it. Cairenes were odd that way, part of a city that loved anything which trumpeted its vaunted modernity.

He had sent Onsi off, despite protestations to stay and help. Hamed had insisted. Who wanted to spend the night after completing their first big case typing up reports? There'd be paperwork enough next week. There was *always* more paperwork. He read over the review he'd written about the Ministry's latest recruit, using words like "commendable" and "exceeds expectations." Maybe this partner thing wouldn't be so bad after all.

Pausing in his work, he picked up the copy of *Al-Masri* he kept nearby. The front of the evening daily read in bold letters: EGYPT'S LADIES GET THE VOTE! Beneath was a photo of two women holding up victory signs. Much of the newspaper was dedicated to the day's big happenings, but Hamed turned several pages to another story.

In a corner at the bottom of page four, a photo showed him and Onsi. Still in their dresses and quite veiled, they stood on either side of the grimacing al. The photographer who had captured the image had promised he'd do his best to see it make the paper. There was no story attached, just the words beneath reading: *Ministry Agents Capture Ramses Station Fiend.* But for Hamed that was more than enough. He smiled as he looked over the grainy image, and pondered whether perhaps he should have it framed. Or would that be too vain? A rap on his door made him hurriedly close the newspaper, looking up to find a familiar but unexpected figure.

Agent Fatma el-Sha'arawi stood in his doorway. She was resplendent as ever, in a lavender Englishman's suit and matching vest with a white shirt and a deep purple tie, topped off with a black bowler no less.

"Good evening, Agent Hamed," she greeted him pleasantly. "Am I bothering you?"

"Evening to you, Agent Fatma," Hamed said, standing and unconsciously straightening his uniform. "And no, not a bother at all. Please, come in." The smaller woman smiled, strolling in on a pair of black and tan wingtips.

Hamed fidgeted at his uniform again.

"I wondered if you were a fan of basbousa?" she asked. Hamed looked to her outstretched hand, only then noticing the small golden cake she held, topped with sugary almonds.

He smiled back with nod. "I love basbousa."

"Great! I thought I'd have to try and eat this all myself." Whipping off her bowler, she hung it on a peg and pulled up a chair to the front of his desk. Hamed cleared a space and found some clean spoons. In moments, the two were digging into the sweet cake that tasted faintly of orange.

"I figured you'd be out celebrating tonight," he said, trying to make appropriate conversation. He couldn't remember the last time they'd spoken more than greetings.

Fatma nodded a head of cropped black curls. "That's what this cake was for. I was supposed to be heading downtown to meet a friend, but had a case that kept me over. And now . . ." She gestured to the report sheets spread about his desk.

"Paperwork," they both said at once.

"What was the case?" he asked, unable to help himself.

She rolled her eyes, digging out another piece of cake. "Some necromancer thought it'd be a brilliant idea to re-animate a sorcerer buried in the Valley of the Kings, hoping to learn some arcane knowledge. Instead, he brings back the corpse of an ancient pharaoh. I mean it's called the Valley of the *Kings* for a reason, right? So, turns out this ancient king is a megalomaniac, and now that he's back, wants to raise an army of the dead from their tombs and conquer the country. Or the world. I forget. Anyway, managed to seal the dead god-emperor back in his sarcophagus and arrested the necromancer. I hope they charge him with stupidity. That took up the whole day." She made a face of disgust, then stopped to look at Hamed inquiringly. "How about you? What was your case about?"

He gaped at her, dazed. God-emperors and armies of the dead?

"We solved a haunting on a tram," he answered, feeling silly for even saying it. He expected her to give him a polite look of feigned interest. But instead, her face lit up.

"That was you? At Ramses Station? In the dress?"

Hamed nodded sheepishly, pulling out the paper and flipping to page four. "The other one's Agent Onsi. One of our new recruits."

Fatma looked over the photo, shaking her head. "Everyone's been trying to figure out who this was. First we heard the story, then it was in the evening paper. Never would have guessed it was you. They say you fought the spirit right there on the station floor with a knife—hand to hand!"

That wasn't precisely what happened, but why dispute? "It was harrowing," he replied.

They spent a long while thereafter, eating cake and talking, trading stories.

" ... so anyway," Hamed related, as they drank some warm mint tea, "there are authorities flying in from Armenia to take the al back. The Ministry wants me to try to recruit one of them to update our records on folklore in the region. There's even talk of Onsi and myself heading up a special unit handling cases on lesser-known supernatural entities."

"Congratulations!" Fatma said, lifting her cup. "To more paperwork!"

Hamed joined her, returning the toast.

"Seems we've all been busy since joining the Ministry," she mused after taking a sip. "Wrapped up in our own cases. We should take some time out—do things like this more often."

"We should," Hamed agreed, and quite meant it. He paused, deciding to take a risk. "There's been some rumors floating about the Ministry about a case of yours this past summer. It's all the new recruits can talk about. Something to do with the Angelic Council ... ?"

Fatma's face went flat, and she stared at him without expression.

"My apologies," he said at once, feeling abashed. "I didn't mean to intrude. I know those files are sealed."

"They *are* sealed, Agent Hamed," she replied in a serious tone. Then she leaned forward, a smirk playing on her lips as she whispered: "And I've been waiting for someone to just come out and ask me so I can tell it anyway! Now, you can't repeat this. You know how those supposed *angels* are about their secrecy. But it all started when I was called in about a dead djinn . . ."

As Hamed listened to the tale with growing awe, he could only think that Onsi was going to hate missing this.

Turn the page for an excerpt from
P. Djèlí Clark's first Tor.com novella,

The Black God's Drums,

available now!

The night in New Orleans always got something going on, ma maman used to say—like this city don't know how to sleep. You want a good look, take the cable-elevator to the top of one of Les Grand Murs, where airships dock on the hour. Them giant iron walls ring the whole Big Miss on either side. Up here you can see New Algiers on the West Bank, its building yards all choked in factory smoke and workmen scurrying round the bones of new-built vessels like ants. Turn around and there's the downtown wards lit up with gas lamps like glittering stars. You can make out the other wall in the east over at Lake Borgne, and a fourth one like a crescent moon up north round Swamp Pontchar-train—what most folk call La Ville Morte, the Dead City.

Les Grand Murs were built by Dutchmen to protect against the storms that come every year. Not the regular hurricanes neither, but them tempêtes noires that turn the skies into night for a whole week. I was born in one of the big ones some thirteen years back in 1871. The walls held in the Big Miss but the rain and winds almost drowned the city anyway, filling it up like a bowl. Ma maman pushed me out her belly in that storm, clinging to a big sweet gum tree in the middle of thunder and lightning. She said I was Oya's child—the goddess of storms, life, death, and rebirth, who came over with her great-grandmaman from Lafrik, and who runs strong in our blood. Ma maman said that's why I take to high places so, looking to ride Oya's wind.

Les Grand Murs is where I call home these days. It's not the finest accommodations: drafty on winter nights and so hot in the summer all you do is lay about in your own sweat. But lots of street kids set up for themselves up here. Better than getting swept into workhouse orphanages or being conscripted to steal for a Thieving Boss.

Me, I marked out a prime spot: an alcove just some ways off from one of the main airship mooring masts. That's where the gangplanks are laid down for disembarking passengers heading into the city. Concealed in my alcove, I can see them all: in every colour and shade, in every sort of dress, talking in more languages than I can count, their voices competing with the rattle of dirigible engines and the hum of ship propellers. It always gets me to thinking on how there's a whole world out there, full of all kinds of people. One day, I dream, I'm going to get on one of those airships. I'll sail away from this city into the clouds and visit all the places there are to visit, and see all the people there are to see. Of course, watching from my alcove is also good for marking out folk too careless with their purses, luggage, and anything else for the taking. Because in New Orleans, you can't survive on just dreams.

My eyes latch onto a little dandy-looking man in a rusty plaid suit, with slicked-back shiny brown hair and a curly moustache. He got a tight grip on his bags, but there's a golden pocket watch dangling on a chain at his side. A clear invitation if I ever seen one. Somebody's bound to snatch it sooner or later—might as well be me.

I'm about to set out to follow him when the world suddenly slows. The air, sounds, everything. It's like somebody grabbed hold of time and stretched her out at both ends. I turn, slow-like, to look out from the wall as a monstrous moon begins to rise into the sky. No, not a moon, I realize in fright—a skull! A great big bone white skull that fills up the night. It pushes itself up past the horizon to cast a shadow over the city underneath, where the gaslights snuff out one by one. I gape at that horrible face, stripped clean of skin or flesh, that stares back with deep empty black sockets and a grin of bared teeth. It's all I can do not to fall to my knees.

"Not real!" I whisper, shutting my eyes to make the apparition go away. I count to ten in my head, whispering all the while: "Not real! Not real! Not real!"

When I open my eyes again, the skull moon is gone. Time has caught up to normal too—the sounds of the night returning in a rush. And the city is there, spread out again: breathing, shining and alive. I release a breath. This was all Oya's doing, I know. The goddess has strange ways of talking. Not the first time I've been sent one of her visions—though never anything so strong. Never anything that felt so real. They're what folk call premonitions: warnings of things about to happen or things soon to come. Most times I can figure them out quick. But a giant skull moon? I got no damn idea what that's supposed to mean.

"You could just talk to me plain," I mutter in irritation. But Oya doesn't answer. She's already humming a song that whistles in my ears. It's about her mother Yemoja leading some lost fishermen to shore. The moon is Yemoja's domain, after all. Giving up, I turn back, hoping to find my mark again—but instead, I'm startled by the sound of footsteps.

My whole body goes still. Not just footsteps but boots, by the way they fall heavy. More than one pair too. I curse at my bad luck, ducking back down into my alcove. I chose this spot special, because it's some ways off from the usual paths people take—just near enough for me to see them, but far enough to keep out of their way. No one ever comes this far out, to this part of the wall. But those steps are getting closer, heading right for me! Cursing my luck twice again, I scramble back to huddle into a far corner of the alcove, where the shadows fall deep. I'm small enough to curl into a ball if I draw my knees up under me. And if I go real still, I might escape without being seen. I might.

I'm expecting constables. Rare to see any of them up here, but could be the city's decided to do a sweep for one reason or the other. Maddi grá coming up, and they like to make everything look respectable to visitors—respectable for New Orleans, anyway. Maybe someone's complained about all the street kids up here picking pockets. Or worse yet, could be the city's workhouses and factories need more small hands to run their machines—machines that seem to delight in stealing fingers. I grit my teeth and ball up my fists as if trying to protect my own fingers, not daring to breathe. Damn sure ain't going to end up in one of those places.

But the figures that enter my alcove aren't constables. They're men, though, about five of them. I can't make them out in the dark, but by their height and the way they walk they have to be men. They're not wearing the telltale blue uniforms of constables though, with the upside-down gold crescent and five-pointed star stitched on their shoulders. These men are wearing dull faded gray uniforms that almost blend into the dark. Their jackets got patches on the front that I recognize right off:

white stars in a blue cross like an X over a bed of red, the letters CSA stitched underneath. The brisk twangs that roll off their tongues are Southern, but like those uniforms, certainly nothing made in New Orleans.

"Alright then," one of them says. "You can get us what we want?"

"Deal already set up, Capitaine," another voice answers, real casual-like. This one's a Cajun. I'd recognize that bayou accent anywhere. I lift my chin off my knees to risk a peek from under the lid of my cap. The one talking that Cajun talk ain't got on a uniform. He's wearing some old brown pants and a red shirt with suspenders. I still can't make out any faces, but can see a mop of white hair on his head almost down to his shoulders. "Dat scientist be here next day, on a morning airship from Haiti. Gonna see to meeting him myself."

My ears perk up at that. A Haitian scientist? Meeting with these men?

"How long we have to wait?" a third voice asks. This one's impatient, almost whining. "Captain, we don't need all this fuss. I say we just snatch him when he gets here. Put him on our ship and fly off. Have him in Charleston in no time."

The Cajun makes a tsking sound. "Ma Lay! Do dat, brudda, and you get de constables involved. Dey gonna cost you mo dan I do. Not how we do tings down here, no."

"Seems all you folk *do* in this city is drink and gamble and eat," the third voice sneers.

The Cajun chuckles. "We like to pass a good time. Make music and babies too."

The first voice, the one both men called Captain, steps in then. Sounds like he's trying to keep things from boiling over. I glance to those black-booted feet, realizing I hadn't pulled my sleeping blanket into the corner with me. That was careless. But nothing I can do about it now. My heart beats faster, hoping none of them steps on it or bothers to look down.

"So after this scientist gets here," the captain is saying, "then what?"

"When he get settled, I set up de meeting between the two of you," the Cajun answers. There's a pause. "You got what he coming all dis way to get? You don't deliver, he might run."

"We got his jewel, alright," the third voice says in his usual sneer.

The Cajun claps, and I imagine him smiling. "Den it should work out fine." He extends a hand and the captain offers over a thick wad of something. The unmistakable beautiful sound of crisp bills being counted fills up my alcove.

"You'll get the rest when we see this scientist—and his invention," the captain states.

"Wi, Capitaine," the Cajun replies. "You give him his jewel and he gonna hand over dat ting you want." He stops his counting and leans in close. "De Black God's Drums. Maybe you boys able to win dis war yet, yeah."

The captain dips his head in a nod before answering. "Maybe."

There's some more talk. Nothing important from what I can tell. Just the questions and assurances of men who don't trust each other and who up to no good. But I'm only half-listening by now. My mind is on the words the Cajun said: the Black God's Drums. With a Haitian scientist involved, that can only mean one thing. And if I'm right, that's big. Bigger than any marks I was going to pinch tonight. This is information that's gonna be valuable to somebody. I just need to figure out who'll pay the highest price. Long after the men leave my alcove, I sit there thinking hard in the dark as Oya hums in my head.

Acknowledgments

Thanks to everyone at Tor.com Publishing who helped make this story a reality, from spark to finish. Big ups as well to the barista at the Kensington coffee spot in London in July 2017, who kept me supplied with "flat whites" to get me through this novella—and put up with my Harry Potter jokes. An extra special debt of gratitude to all the readers of "A Dead Djinn in Cairo," who kept asking for "more" from this world. Hope this delivers.

About the Author

Born in New York and raised mostly in Houston, **P. DJÈLÍ CLARK** spent the formative years of his life in the homeland of his parents, Trinidad and Tobago. His writing has appeared in *Daily Science Fiction, Heroic Fantasy Quarterly, Lightspeed, Tor.com,* and print anthologies including *Griots* I and II, *Steamfunk, Myriad Lands Volume 2,* and *Hidden Youth.* He is also the author of the Tor.com novella *The Black God's Drums.* He currently resides in a small castle in Hartford, Connecticut, with his wife, two infant daughters, and a rambunctious Boston terrier.

pdjeliclark.wordpress.com

twitter.com/pdjeliclark

TOR·COM

**Science fiction. Fantasy. The universe.
And related subjects.**

*

More than just a publisher's website, *Tor.com*
is a venue for **original fiction, comics,** and
discussion of the entire field of SF and fantasy,
in all media and from all sources. Visit our site
today—and join the conversation yourself.